KT-365-471

The

WAY PAST WINTER

Chicken House

2 Palmer Street, Frome, Somerset BA11 1DS
chickenhousebooks.com

Kiran Millwood Hargrave

First published in Great Britain in 2018
Chicken House
2 Palmer Street
Frome, Somerset BA11 1DS
United Kingdom
www.chickenhousebooks.com

Cover and interior design by Helen Crawford-White
Typeset by Dorchester Typesetting Group Ltd
Printed and bound in Great Britain by CPI Group (UK) Ltd, Croydon CR0 4YY

The paper used in this Chicken House book is made from
wood grown in sustainable forests.

1 3 5 7 9 10 8 6 4 2

British Library Cataloguing in Publication data available.

HB ISBN 978-1-911077-93-0
eISBN 978-1-911490-35-7

'Kiran is such a beautiful, sparkling writer. This gorgeous story of bravery, sisterhood, goodbyes and beginnings is a must for everyone.'
JESSIE BURTON

'Exquisitely woven and beautifully atmospheric.' **ABI ELPHINSTONE**

'Kiran Millwood Hargrave has written another classic in the making. No end of love for her brave girls, big adventures, beautiful writing, and gorgeous settings.' **SAMANTHA SHANNON**

'Such a delicately crafted, timely fairy tale. The words just sing, as if every sentence is poetry. Read it – and fall beneath its wintry spell.'
CERRIE BURNELL

'This mesmeric tale of three gutsy sisters on a vital quest contains some of the most exquisite descriptions of snow I've ever read!'
EMMA CARROLL

'A white-knuckle ride of ice and snow that will also melt even the coldest heart.' **PIERS TORDAY**

'Gorgeous, heartfelt and incredibly exciting. Her best yet, and that's saying something.' **ROBIN STEVENS**

'Dazzling! A heart-sledging, goosebump-tingling adventure with enough warmth to melt an endless winter.' **SOPHIE ANDERSON**

'A gorgeous snowy adventure that feels like a familiar fairy tale told in a new way. I loved it and can't wait for everyone to discover *The Way Past Winter*.' **KATHERINE WEBBER**

'An ice-cold adventure with the warmest of hearts, and I loved it.'
ROSS WELFORD

'Spellbinding. *The Way Past Winter* has whisked me away to a land of snow-deep forests. Glorious.' **KATHERINE WOODFINE**

I n *The Way Past Winter*, Kiran writes 'stories are just a different way of telling the truth' – and the truth is exactly what you'll find in her most poignant story yet. We start with a winter that threatens to stay for ever, and a family undone. In order to find healing, three sisters must face a deep and frightening truth about their relationship with the natural world – and perhaps our own. Awesome, exciting and full of rich images that will always stay with me, this is classic storytelling by a brilliantly talented writer.

BARRY CUNNINGHAM
Publisher
Chicken House

For N, & my brother John,
the brave ones

Also by Kiran Millwood Hargrave

The Girl of Ink & Stars
The Island at the End of Everything

Part 1
HOME

Chapter One

The House in Eldbjørn Forest

I t was a winter they would tell tales about. A winter that arrived so sudden and sharp it stuck birds to branches, and caught the rivers in such a frost their spray froze and scattered down like clouded crystals on the stilled water. A winter that came, and never left.

Three years passed, then five. People spoke of curses and offered up prayers and promises. They blamed mages, their neighbours, the jarls who ruled their villages and towns. But blame didn't break the winter, and soon no one could remember warmth except from fire, or green apart from the silvery hue of the fir trees.

Carts were abandoned in favour of sleighs, fine horses lost their worth until they were all traded for mountain ponies or mewling husky pups, or other animals that knew snow. Bears sank into perpetual hibernation, wolves slunk into the shadows of the vast forest. Some folk moved from their frozen land, but most stayed and, as people do, changed to fit their changed world.

They changed their stories too. Gone were tellings of honey and plenty: tales became warnings, sharp as bee stings. The fire-geese who bore the sun on their backs in summer became ice-swans who nip at exposed fingers and toes, snapping them clean off. The river nymphs became ice maidens who stalk the bottom of frozen lakes, waiting to pull wayward children under. Wistful voices spoke of magical islands where spring waited, of waterfalls of gold streaming into pools of sunlight, but always these places were beyond reach, just past the frozen horizon.

In the winter's fifth year, its grip still tightening on the southern river towns and northern mountain cities, a whole new order of cold wove itself tight as a basket about the families that lived in the remotest parts of the land. And it was in a small house tucked in a narrow pocket of forest rimed with snow thigh-deep, that three sisters and their brother were having a disagreement over a cabbage.

'Please don't boil it again, Sanna,' pleaded Pípa, the youngest. She sat shivering, her hands over her cold ears, lip wobbling as she regarded the shrivelled, hard-leafed vegetable. 'We have had nothing but boiled all week.'

'I'll not be told what to do by a child not even old

enough for her given name,' said Sanna briskly, like a superstitious woman thrice her seventeen years might, for Pípa was seven. It would be another year before they could be sure the evil eye had passed over her, and she was regifted her true name. 'And besides, it's the way to get the most good out.'

She stood with her cutting knife hovering, looking for the best incision point for the particularly hard and meagre cabbage.

'There's dripping,' said Mila hopefully, trying not to echo the whine of her little sister. 'We could fry—'

'And use up firewood to get the dripping hot enough?' chided Oskar from his spot furthest from the fire. 'We must boil it. Grow up, Pípa. I've had enough of your trembling lip.'

'Leave her, Oskar,' said Mila, wrapping her arm around Pípa and frowning at their big brother. He was nothing like he used to be before Papa left: he was becoming a stranger. Now he spoke only to thank their eldest sister Sanna for the food she gave him each morning before he waded into the thigh-high snow to check his traps, or to tell one of his little sisters off.

Mila caught up Pípa's stiff fingers and blew her hot breath on to them. 'Come, Píp, let's not trouble Sanna – she knows her cabbages.'

'That I do!' said Sanna, having located the cabbage's weakest point and bringing the knife down with a satisfying *thwack*. 'Boiled it is.'

Outside, one of the dogs started to bark. Mila knew it was Dusha – her voice was higher than her brother's, more whiny and insistent, like Pípa's. A moment later it was joined by Danya's whip-crack yowl.

'Those dogs!' huffed Sanna. 'Oskar—'

But Mila was already on her feet, taking her fur-lined boots from beside the fire. 'I'll go.'

She threw on her russet cloak and wrapped her fox fur around her brown hair, but before she could unbolt the door someone knocked twice, and then twice more, in a jaunty rhythm that had become familiar to the family over the past months.

'Wait!' called Sanna, but Mila grinned mischievously and drew the bolt. She heard her sister swear loudly and clatter the saucepans, searching for the copper one that they sometimes used as a mirror.

A mountain pony was tied to the mounting post in the yard and a boy stood before Mila. He was Sanna's age and Oskar's height, with a plump, handsome face, fair where all the Oreksons were dark. He flushed when he saw Mila's teasing smile.

'Back again, Geir?' said Mila. 'I didn't know we'd sent

any knives for sharpening this week.'

'Just the one,' said Geir, as Mila heard Sanna skidding into place behind her. Mila looked up at her big sister from under her fox fur and waggled her eyebrows. Sanna had let her hair down and pinched her cheeks into a rosy flush. She'd even bitten her lips in an effort to redden them and she'd broken the skin slightly on the lower one. She pulled Mila out of the way with a pincer grip.

'Hello, Geir.' Sanna's voice was oddly husky, as if she had a cold.

'Hello, Sanna,' squeaked Geir.

Mila snorted and stomped her way back to the kitchen, pulling the door closed behind her to keep the warmth in. They'd grown used to the pathetic exchanges that passed for conversation between their sister and the knife-sharpener from Stavgar.

Oskar looked up from where he was finishing slicing Sanna's cabbage with his hunting knife. Its handle was intricately carved to look like roots twisted across it, and it had a thick blade, better suited to cutting rope and wood than vegetables. 'Geir again?'

'Yep,' said Mila, removing her hat and rolling her eyes.

'Were they kissing?' giggled Pípa.

'Pípa!' scolded Oskar. 'Don't be ridiculous.' He looked sharply at Mila. 'They weren't, were they?' His hand tightened on the knife.

Mila thought about teasing him, but then her stomach rumbled. She didn't have the energy. 'Of course not. He's just bringing a knife.'

'Another one?'

'Mmm.' She collapsed on the bench beside the fire, watching the steam rising from the water that would soon be the same thin greyish cabbage soup they'd eaten for weeks now.

Mila listened to the knife ripping through the cabbage and strained to hear the murmurs of Sanna and Geir's exchange. The lovely bell of Sanna's laugh rang out before the front door closed with a creak and a bang, blowing the kitchen door open and sending cold fingers of wind raking across Mila's cheeks. Sanna floated in, a faraway look on her thin face as she gazed at something in her palm.

'What's that?' asked Pípa.

'Nothing,' said Sanna hurriedly, pinning the some-thing, gleaming, into her cloak. 'A gift.' It was a brooch, intricately worked from elk horn, full of pale swirls that recalled a foaming sea. It was very fine.

'And what did you give in return?' asked Mila, bring-ing vivid spots of red to her sister's cheeks.

'Nothing,' said Sanna briskly, brandishing the newly

sharpened knife mock-threateningly at Mila. 'A gift shouldn't be given with the expectation of something in return.'

'That's the fourth time he's been round in a week,' said Oskar.

'Hmm,' said Sanna, purse-lipped.

'It's a long way from Stavgar, he'll be riding back in the dark.'

'Hmm.'

'Perhaps next time you could invite him in for dinner?'

Mila saw a look pass between her older siblings, full of something she didn't understand.

'Yes,' said Sanna. 'Maybe I will.' She swallowed, then said in a firm tone that meant the subject was closed, 'Now, are you done butchering that cabbage?'

The dim day fell into the dark lap of dusk, and the small house filled with the smell of boiled cabbage soup that meant dinner was ready. Sanna was just about to ladle Pípa's portion into a chipped wooden bowl when Dusha set about barking, followed by her brother.

'Not Geir again?' said Oskar, and Sanna shook her head.

'Probably just spooked. I'll go and calm them,' said Mila, in no hurry for her bowl of soup, despite her

9

hunger. She put on her cloak and hat for the second time, opened the door a crack and stepped into the snow, which glowed a silvery grey in the uncertain light.

'Coming, Dush-Dush! Coming, Danya!'

Keeping her head bowed against the biting wind, she heaved the door closed behind her and began to trudge through the drifts towards the dog shed with its wooden gate, hands tucked under her armpits to keep them warm. But she had not taken more than three steps before she collided with something.

'*Javoyt!*' Mila stumbled back, standing on her cloak, and nearly fell. She regained her balance and looked up. Her heart thudded almost as loud as the wind. Now she knew why the dogs were barking.

Chapter Two

The Stranger

'Man's language from such a little girl,' said a voice, deep and punchy as Danya's barks, which grew louder. 'What is your name?'

Mila pulled her scarf up to cover her lips, swallowing down a fearful tang as she smelt a horrifying, animal scent, bitter as rotten leaves. Before her stood a horse, as square and as huge, it seemed to her, as a barn. On its back sat a man so swathed in fur he looked as large as the horse. A woodcutter's axe like her father's glinted at his waist, and his eyes flashed gold and wild above shadowy stubble.

Behind him were a dozen smaller figures on ponies, cloaked and hooded and bearing torches. One of them carried a pennant, embroidered, Mila saw, with a bear beneath a tree. Gold stitches glinted at its roots in the torchlight.

From all of them there lifted a steam of heat, and the

ponies were snorting and stamping, shying away from the dogs, who were throwing themselves at the gate. The man raised a hand, and both animals fell silent, collapsing on the ground like emptied sails.

'No!' Mila wrenched her feet from where they seemed frozen in the snow. 'Dush! Dan—'

But the dogs were only lying quietly, noses resting on their forepaws, eyebrows twitching above wide-open eyes. Even the trees behind them seemed to still.

Mila turned cautiously back to the assembled company. She peered past the man at the next rider. His chin was unstubbled, as if he were a boy of Oskar's age. Perhaps he was this man's son? She looked into the next face, then the next. All the riders were boys, some perhaps only a year older than she. Surely he could not have so many sons?

Her voice was caught in her throat, fluttering like a captured bird. The man swung his huge leg over the back of the horse and landed in the snow. No, that wasn't quite right . . .

Mila stared at the man's feet. He wore fine, unscuffed black leather boots that showed no signs of a hard journey, but that was not what made her stare.

The man had not landed in the snow – he had landed on it. He hadn't sunk into the soft powder, although she could feel it seeping over the tops of her boots, and his companions' ponies were in almost to their hocks.

Mila dragged her head up and saw he was looking directly at her, with those fierce eyes. When Mila again looked down, he was up to his calves in snow. What's more, his fine boots were now tied about his calves with lengths of golden cord, like the tree roots on the pennant.

Mila blinked, and the man smiled, baring teeth grey and slabbed as charred wood. She swallowed, bitterness rising like a tide beneath her tongue.

'Winter-well-met,' said the man, pausing for her to return the greeting, which she did not. 'Aren't you going to welcome us?'

'I . . .' Mila cleared her throat and tried again. 'I do not know you.'

The man gave a laugh as clipped as his voice. 'And I do not know you, child. But where I am from we always welcome a visitor who comes, tired, to our door.'

'Mila?'

She spun around. She had not heard the door open, but now Oskar, without a cloak or a fur, his boots unlaced, was pulling it to behind him. Beyond him, Mila saw the distorted faces of her sisters pressed against the ice-filled window like twin moons.

'Mila, is it?' murmured the man. Mila felt a tightening

behind her eyes, like the beginnings of a headache. She wished Oskar had not said her name.

Her brother approached as he might a circling wolf, wading carefully through the snow drifts and placing himself between Mila and the man. He pushed her back slightly, and she knew he wanted her to go inside, but she did not want to leave him alone with them. His slight frame and bare head only made the man's bulk seem more overwhelming: a sapling set before an ancient oak.

'Who are you?' said Oskar, his back straight, voice louder than it needed to be. Mila noticed that the wind seemed to have quietened, and though the trees were unnaturally still, Oskar's dark hair was blowing about his ears.

'I would speak to the man of the house,' said the man, his golden gaze set over Oskar's head.

'I am he,' said Oskar.

'Really? Where is your father?'

Mila felt a lump rise in her throat, and heard the same tightness in Oskar's voice as he replied, 'Gone.'

'How old are you?'

'Fifteen years of winter.'

'And your name?'

'Oskar.'

'Oskar,' repeated the man, a cruel smile playing about

14

his stubbled cheeks. 'Winter-well-met, Oskar. As I was about to tell Mila –' the tightness behind her eyes ratcheted – 'we are come from the south. We've been trading.'

'Trading what?'

'Treasure.' The man grinned and clicked his fingers. His companions pulled their cloaks up so the golden cord about their ankles was more clearly revealed. Mila had never seen gold worked in such a way, spun into thin, flexible strands. But the result was not exactly beautiful. It was knotted and rough looking, like the roots carved on Oskar's knife. Ugly and fine, like the stranger.

Oskar took a wondering step towards them, and as one the men dropped their cloaks again.

'Where are you taking such riches?'

'North.' A look at the man's face told Mila that Oskar would not be getting more information than that, but she knew there was not much north: only the mountain city of Bovnik and the Boreal Sea, with its stories of magical islands where spring still lived.

'What business have you in Bovnik?' asked Oskar.

'Our own,' sneered the man, his voice harsher than before. 'We hope for food, and permission to start a fire and pass the night.'

After a moment's hesitation, Oskar replied, 'I am not sure we can give it.'

The man took a step forward, and Mila's heart swelled with pride as Oskar gave only the smallest of flinches.

'What did you say, boy?'

'Winter is falling harder lately,' said Oskar. 'And the forest is less giving by the day—'

'We are well aware, having ridden its veins,' spat the man. 'And perhaps it is only that the forest has given enough.'

Oskar swallowed, then continued, 'We have no food to spare. I cannot risk my family.'

'Ah. So there are more of you?'

A stab of foreboding pierced Mila's chest. *Do not answer him*, she willed Oskar. The man flicked his gaze to her for a moment, almost as if he'd heard her. But Oskar, seeming to think the man was softening, plunged on.

'Yes. Sanna, Pípa and Mila. I have three sisters.'

'Three? What a curse.' The others laughed again, and Mila bristled as Oskar joined in half-heartedly. 'But such pretty names.'

Oskar stopped laughing, face suddenly fearful. 'So, you see, I cannot risk running short of food.'

'So, I do see,' crooned the man. 'But surely you cannot begrudge us some ground, some dry moss to start our fire?'

'Of course,' said Oskar. 'I'll return with the moss.' His

shoulders slumped and he turned back towards her. 'Come, Mila.'

'Goodnight, Mila,' called the man.

The pain spiked her temples once more as she stepped over the threshold and Oskar closed the door behind them. Mila released the breath she had been holding and shuddered. She knew she would not sleep well with such wildness so close by.

'What happened?' Pípa gabbled. Oskar was shivering, and Sanna knelt to take his boots off. 'Who were they?'

But Oskar only waved Sanna away and drew Mila to him, rubbing her shoulders before sweeping her into a tight hug. 'Are you all right, Milenka?'

Mila leant into her big brother. It had been so long since he had called her that, or held any of them. Since Papa had walked into the white, five winter years before, Oskar had grown up so fast it seemed he had left loving them behind, just as Papa had.

'Yes,' she murmured.

Oskar gave her a final squeeze and released her. 'Good. Now none of you speak to them, all right? I'll take some moss to them, and then we stay inside until they are gone. None of you go out tomorrow until I give the all-clear. Agreed?'

Even Sanna, who hated taking orders from her

younger brother, nodded. Mila turned her head to the iced window, and fancied she saw a shadow twitch away. The man had not told them his name. He had her brother's and sisters' names, though. He had hers.

Chapter Three

A Face at the Ice Window

M any hours later, something woke Mila, bringing her up from a deep sleep, gasping. She lay still as her heartbeat slowed, listening to the sounds of her sleeping family. She liked this about living in constant winter: they all slept in the kitchen together, on pallets by the fire for warmth. Sanna, who had been twelve when the winter began, spoke longingly of how she'd once had her own bedroom for summer, with the thinnest cotton curtains, but now the door to the summer rooms, with their thinner walls and larger windows, was boarded up. Besides, Mila could not imagine sleeping alone.

Pípa's light snuffles were close to her ear, and Sanna's deep sighing breaths were on her other side, her wing of raven-blue-black hair encroaching as always on to her straw pillow. But from the other side of her big sister, Oskar's shallow breaths were missing.

Mila sat up carefully, the heavy furs sliding off her. Instantly she was cold, though she was stitched tight into her new winter vest, restuffed with moss by Sanna only last week. Even this close to the fire, her breath made little puffs, like a dragon from one of Papa's stories.

Papa. Mila breathed the word to herself, for the first time in months. There was a sort of unspoken rule between them that they did not talk about him, though he was everywhere in the house, from the trousers Oskar had recently grown into, to his woodcutter's axes lying beside the fire, handles smooth with use.

But the stranger asking about his whereabouts had brought memories rushing back. She remembered so much it was painful. He'd smelt of sap and woodsmoke. His eyes were ice-blue chips, like Sanna's. He'd had a wild laugh and a wilder heart, but it was kind, too. Not even her papa had been wild in the way that man outside was.

She felt empty, like a hand that is dropped when it is used to being held, and, for the first time in ages, she wanted to do things that brought him closer, rather than pushing him further away. Maybe tomorrow, when the stranger and his boys had gone, they could go to the heart tree, and sit and tell stories, like they used to.

She thought of the bear stitched on the man's pennant. Papa had told stories about Bjørn, the bear spirit who protects trees, and Eld, the lonely bear who fell in love with the sun. Sad, lovely stories, nothing like the stranger.

Mila looked towards the dark ice window, and had to clap a hand to her mouth to keep from screaming. A face, distorted and huge, was at the window. It was illuminated grotesquely by the fire, which made it broad and beastly, stretched as though it had no solid edges. Gold eyes glinted in the flickering light. And standing before the window—

'Oskar?' Mila whispered.

The stranger's face disappeared, and Oskar turned from where he had stood looking out. Mila slipped out of bed and went to him, bare feet cringing at the fierce cold of the floor where the rushes had grown thin. She stopped just short of touching him. Their hug seemed a lifetime ago; now distance stretched between them. His face seemed drained of blood, his eyes large and glassy.

'Oskar, what are you doing?'

'I was watching the men.' Oskar's voice was quiet, harsh.

'What are they doing?'

'Nothing.'

Mila craned to see past him. 'You were talking to him.'

'No, I wasn't.' Oskar shifted to block her view. There was a sheen of sweat on his upper lip. He looked feverish.

'Do you need some broth? Shall I wake Sanna?'

'No,' he said, barely containing his anger. 'Go back to bed.'

Mila jutted her chin and narrowed her eyes at him. 'What's going on?'

A shadow, like an eel flickering under the surface of a lake, shifted in her brother's face. He looked suddenly older. He looked . . . not himself.

Mila reached up to touch the strange bulge of her brother's cheek, but he grasped her wrist in a rough clasp, fingers cold on her bed-warm skin. She gasped and tears started in her eyes at the sudden hurt of it. He leant closer. 'Go back to sleep, Mila.'

A stab of pain at her temple joined the ache in her wrist as he released her. Chest heaving, Mila did as she was told, sliding quickly between her sisters, and pulling the furs up over her head, trying to control her breathing. A small hand found hers, and she realized Pípa was awake too. She shuffled her covers until her little sister's wide eyes shone at her in the dark.

'What's wrong with Oskar?' whispered Pípa.

Mila only held a finger to her lips. She did not want their brother – or the stranger – to hear them.

22

Chapter Four

Gone

'U p!'
The furs were pulled roughly off Mila. She cried out, raising her fists to protect herself, but it was only Sanna.

'Get up, Mila. Come on.' The light was the pale grey of morning, and her elder sister was dressed in her work dress, Geir's brooch pinned over her heart, her black hair pulled back into a severe bun. Her eyes were narrowed, her jaw tense with irritation.

'What's—?' started Pípa blearily, her hand still wrapped around Mila's fingers.

'The men are gone,' said Sanna sharply.

'That's good,' said Mila, shivering and attempting to pull the covers back over herself.

Sanna let out a brief, bitter laugh. 'So is our brother.'

Mila felt an icicle of fear stab her chest.

'Oskar is gone?' squeaked Pípa.

Mila rubbed her eyes, trying to make her brain wake up faster. 'Perhaps he followed them to the Stavgar boundary to see that they really have left? Or to the heart tree—'

Sanna looked at her sharply. 'Why would he go there?'

'The man,' started Mila, hesitantly. 'Yesterday, he asked where our father was, and . . . it made me think of Papa. Maybe Oskar went there because it made him think about him too.'

'Oskar told us not to go there,' said Pípa seriously.

'You know he doesn't listen to anyone's advice, not even his own,' said Mila. 'Or maybe he went to check the traps early?'

Sanna rolled her eyes, and the icicle in Mila's chest melted slightly into a trickle of annoyance. Why was Sanna not more worried?

'Should we go and check?' Mila said, bracing herself against the morning chill and hurrying over to the fire, where her tunic hung. She slid it over her head and wove her belt around her waist three times, knotting it at the side before pulling on her wool leggings. They were warm and smoky, and she took a deep breath, calming herself. 'I can take Dusha and the sleigh—'

Sanna let out another strange, hiccuping laugh. Mila rounded on her. 'What's so funny?'

'It's not funny at all,' said Sanna, taking a deep breath and setting her shoulders square. She looked very beautiful, Mila thought through her anger, and very distant. 'But we should have seen it coming.'

'Seen what coming?' said Pípa, but Sanna just swung around and took the snow bucket from its hook beside the fire.

'I'm going for fresh snow. Lay rushes – they're getting patchy in here.'

'What should we have seen?' asked Pípa, but Mila only shook her head. Mention of the rushes had brought back the memory of her bare feet on the freezing dirt floor, her strange exchange with Oskar.

'I saw something last night,' said Mila. 'Oskar was standing by the window. He was talking to someone outside, I think—'

Sanna stiffened, and on her face was a look Mila had no name for. 'The ice is inches thick. You can't hear through it.'

'Well, he was watching someone, then. And they were watching him back.'

Sanna turned away quickly, but Mila thought she saw her face crumple slightly. 'Go and get the rushes.'

'Can't I look for him? He looked strange, like—'

'It sounds like a dream to me,' said her sister sharply.

'Do as I say.'

She flung her shawl over her head, and left the kitchen. A moment later they heard the wind howl, and a gust of winter air puffed through the kitchen, making the fire flicker, before Sanna closed the door behind her.

Mila knew that voice: there was no point arguing. She opened the door to the store and reached up for the rushes where they hung drying on a hook. Her sleeves slid back and she saw a livid bruise around one wrist, purple and blue as a thundercloud. *It wasn't a dream*, she thought. There was a rustle behind her and she turned to see Pípa, still in her nightclothes, fur slippers on her feet.

'Come, Píp. Get dressed, and then you can help me lay the floor.'

Sanna swept in with the fresh snow as they left the store, and was too slow wiping her eyes.

'Why are you crying?' said Pípa.

Sanna grimaced. 'I'm not.' She slammed the door behind her. Her pale cheeks were flushed with cold, her huge eyes stark. 'Stop *staring* at me, Pípa.'

'Were there tracks? Did you see which way—?' started Mila, but Sanna shook her head.

'Only an animal's,' she said curtly. 'Otherwise it's snow-smooth. Like they were never here at all.'

She stomped to the kitchen to hang the bucket over

the fire to melt. Mila went to the front door and opened it a small crack. Sanna hadn't lied – the yard was unblemished aside from Sanna's dragging tracks looping from the door; there were chopping block-sized imprints, too big to be an elk or a wolf, circling the boundary, disappearing around the side of the house and out of Mila's sight. *North*.

'All gone?' asked Pípa, trying to peer past her.

Mila nodded, swallowing hard. She couldn't understand why Sanna wouldn't let her go and see where Oskar was. Pípa leant into her waist. 'Can I put on my day clothes later? When Oskar comes back?'

Mila nodded. 'We'll start with the food store. We can do the kitchen after breakfast when . . . when he's home.'

But even after they had relaid the rushes in the food store, the kitchen and the corridor, Oskar had not returned.

'He'll have gone straight to the traps,' said Mila, more to comfort herself than Pípa.

'Without breakfast?'

'The boundary, then—'

'Without Danya?' interrupted Sanna tersely. 'He never goes into the forest without that dog. He went with *them*.'

Mila wanted to shake her. 'What?'

'Isn't it obvious?' said Sanna, speaking as though to a

small and stupid child. 'He went with them.'

'Why would he do that? He wouldn't,' said Mila, suddenly feeling very hot.

'Why not? Why not choose adventures over three sisters? Over – what did he say that man called us? – a *curse*.'

'Oskar loves us,' said Pípa, her lower lip wobbling. 'He wouldn't go away.'

Sanna laughed hollowly. 'Oh, yes, Oskar loves us, just like Papa loved us, just like Mama—'

'They did love us!' cried Mila, feeling as though she'd been punched.

But Sanna's eyes were wild and bright. 'Papa loved us so much he left us, walked out and never looked back. And now Oskar has done the same.'

Mila's breath was coming in little stabs, like a stitch. They never talked about how Papa left, how he rose early on the anniversary of Mama's death and walked into the winter without a hat or cloak. 'You don't know that. Oskar says Papa loved us, only he loved Mama more. He couldn't live here without her—'

'She was already gone!' Sanna was on her feet, shouting now. Mila saw spit flying from her mouth, and threw an anxious glance at Pípa. Mama had died giving birth to her, and they were careful not to talk about it much. 'He was following her, but she was already years dead. He preferred to leave his family in the hands of our fickle brother, who ran as soon as a better offer came along—'

The heat in Mila expanded, making her hands tingle and pulling her to her feet, too. 'He wouldn't leave. He must have been taken.'

'I heard no struggle. No sign of the door being forced, no blood in the snow,' Sanna said, breathing raggedly. 'Did you?'

'There was something wrong with that man who was leading them, something bad.' Mila thought of his feet on the snow, the way he silenced the dogs with a gesture. 'Something dangerous.'

'Perhaps where you saw danger, Oskar saw excitement,' said Sanna, quieter now. She stood, her shoulders slumped, long neck dipped, and Mila could see her nails digging into her palms. 'And I don't blame him. If I were a man, I'd leave. I'd walk out that door and never come back.'

Mila felt the breath knocked from her chest. Pípa ran forward to cling to Sanna's skirts. 'Don't go, San.'

Sanna pushed her away roughly and gave another mirthless laugh. 'I won't.' She looked up and her eyes were bright with tears. 'I've nowhere to go.'

She threw her cloak over her shoulders, and a moment

later they heard the door slam and the dogs begin to bark. Mila knew she was going to sit with them in the dog shed. It was what any of them did when they were upset.

She felt as though the floor had turned to snow slush beneath her feet, and sat down hard on the bench. Pípa was crying quietly, and Mila pulled her on to her lap, rocking her gently.

'Is . . . she . . . leaving?' said Pípa, hiccuping.

'No, she's only gone to sulk with the dogs. Hear them whining with her?' said Mila, in the brightest voice she could manage.

'So . . .' began Pípa. 'You don't think Oskar left us? He's coming back?'

Mila pressed her face into Pípa's thick braid, thinking hard. 'I'll go and look for him. It'll be fast with both dogs. I'll check the traps, the heart tree. He might be hurt or . . .' She swallowed. 'I'll be back before full-dark if I leave now.'

'Can I come?'

'Absolutely not.' She patted Pípa to signal she wanted to get up. 'I had better tell Sanna I'm going.'

Mila wrapped herself in her cloak and hat, and paused a moment before grabbing Sanna's too – she'd rather let her freeze for her meanness. She gave Pípa another quick hug before heading to the dog shed.

It was a low turf-roofed structure, always warm, even in winter. In a rare memory of her mother, Mila remembered her teasing Papa: *You spoil those dogs. It's better built than our own home!* It was true, in part: all the gaps in the walls were plugged with straw for extra protection against the wind, and the roof was double thickness. Mila took a deep breath as she entered, inhaling the warm biscuity smell of the dogs, so comforting even in her saddest moments.

Sanna was squeezed into a dark corner, Danya bundled across her lap, Dusha lying alongside. Mila felt her temper subside, seeing her big sister, normally so composed, crumpled like a pile of rags beneath the dogs.

'I'm going to the heart tree, and to check the traps.'

'What's the use?' said Sanna, voice thick, as she extricated her hand from beneath Danya's chin. The dog gave a whining complaint, twitching his muzzle at her.

'He's gone, Mila. Just like Papa.' She drew something out from the deer-hide pouch on her day belt. 'I found this in the doorway when I fetched the snow.'

In her palm lay their father's ring: dull bronze set with a large garnet, smoky and smooth from years of constant wear. Mila took it, scarcely breathing.

Their mother had given him that stone, quarried from

the mine where she worked in Bovnik when he asked her to handfasten with him. In a clear, shining moment of memory, Mila remembered her father worrying at the ring after lighting the wick in a dish of cold deer fat on the anniversary of their mother's death. *To bring her memory into the light.*

An awful sadness enveloped her worry for Oskar, like a heavy net closing over a shoal of panicking fish. *Papa.* His broad, bearded face, thumb working at the garnet, rubbing it to a shine, his ice-blue eyes desperate . . .

And the next day, he was gone. Oskar had called for his sisters and gone rushing into the snow-hushed forest, come back almost a day later, the ring clenched in his hand, scratched to pieces and crying. *He's gone. He's gone.* When he'd calmed, he told them how he'd scoured the forest.

I found this by the heart tree, he'd finished, opening his palm to show the ring, which had left grooves in his skin.

Did you look in the tree? Are you sure Papa didn't just climb it? asked Mila. *Maybe he went to remember Mama.*

Oskar had fixed her with a look so haunted she'd paled in terror.

What is it?

He wasn't there. And we can never go back to the heart tree, he'd said, in a voice as deadened as his eyes. *Promise me.*

They all promised. And as though to keep them caught in the awful memory of that day, the winter stretched and stretched. It was like Papa had taken spring with him, had left them in the cold.

'Mila?'

Mila felt a dread start to fill her throat as she looked from Sanna's face – the same high cheekbones, the same eyes as Papa's – to the ring and back again. She drew back, shaking her head. 'Oskar wouldn't leave it behind. Perhaps he was struggling with them. Perhaps it fell off his finger—'

Sanna gave a sad smile. 'It was in the centre of the doorway, Mila. Placed there, for us to find. It's a message.'

Mila shook her head even harder, setting the ear flaps of her hat dancing. But even as she did so, the first seed of doubt planted itself in the pit of her stomach. She pushed it down, covering it over, making her voice strong and certain.

'I'm going to the heart tree.' She held out the ring and Sanna's hat and cloak. 'I'm taking the dogs, so you'll need these to keep warm out here.'

Sanna sighed, and slid the ring back into the pouch on her belt. She gently pushed Danya off her and stood up, reaching for her cloak. 'I'm coming with you.'

'What about Pípa?'

Sanna hesitated for a moment, as if she'd forgotten there were only three of them now. 'Go and fetch her. Bring some food too. I'll harness the dogs.'

Mila released a breath she didn't know she'd been holding. Though she loved the forest, she hadn't been looking forward to sleighing for a whole day alone. As she trudged back to the house, she scanned the encircling tracks and, beyond them, the larch trees. Bare and pale as bones, they swayed in the icy wind, and seemed to stare back.

Chapter Five

Traps

Mila's cheeks sang with cold, a cold that reached long fingers down inside her throat and up her nose with every breath. Dusha and Danya were doing well, pulling them fast through the snow, driven by a worrisome energy Mila felt under her own skin: a dark fizzing, like a hot coal spitting. She and Sanna kept up the rhythm, pushing with their feet off the snow to help the dogs along, both of them ducking down, then swooping up.

The sleigh was running as well as the dogs. Made of light, unpainted birch, Oskar had renewed the iron on the bottom of the runners only the month before. He'd cut himself, he'd made them so sharp. There were two driving bars, one at the front and one at the back, with planks to stand on. Pípa sat in the wide sealskin bed, braid flying, while Sanna and Mila stood at the back for better balance, keeping the reins loose and long.

They passed the first four traps without slowing: three hare snares beneath a light dusting of snow and leaves, the bait frozen, and one deadfall set at the right height for foxes, who were too clever to step on disturbed ground. Oskar was catching less and less, and Mila thought of what the man had said: *Perhaps it is only that the forest has given enough.* She shuddered.

Their father had laid the traps as straight as the trees would allow, a direct path to his favourite place, and Mila imagined Oskar scuffling to check them, further and further into the forest. But he was not here now, nor was there any sign he had been since the night's snowfall.

She chewed the inside of her cheek. What little of Sanna's face she could see was taut, her lips a dark line. Mila wanted to slide her hand along the bar, to grasp her sister's, but she didn't want to risk losing her grip. Besides, she was still annoyed at her for thinking Oskar would leave willingly, and for saying she would leave too if she had the chance.

A twist of bitterness spiked her stomach as Mila ducked low beneath a grasping branch, feeling it catch momentarily on her cap before whistling past her ear. They passed half a dozen more snares and two pitfalls before the forest started its true gathering together, the trees closer, the pale sky more and more a far-off thought, puzzled to pieces through closing branches.

She could remember a distant spring, before Pípa was born, even before her own name-gifting, when they had walked this same path. Her father had hoisted her on to his back, low-hanging leaves brushing her head. They'd passed through a wall of close trunks, and there in front of them was a mighty birch: the heart tree. It grew unnaturally broad, more akin to an oak, as wide as their house and as high, it seemed to Mila, as the sky. Its leaves formed a blanket over their heads, moss carpeting their steps. Wild flowers grew in the patches of sun, bright splotches of red and purple that threw up a honeyed scent.

Papa had set her gently down. *Race you.*

They'd climbed, all of them breathless and laughing, higher and higher, Oskar and Sanna recklessly fast. Mila's heart pounded but she wasn't afraid, not with Mama close behind. It was a perfect climbing tree, the whorls of the bark soft but strong, fitting her small hands exactly.

When they reached the top, all Mila could see was forest, her whole world a tangle of wood and leaves. She had never felt so happy.

This is the most special place in all the forest, said Mama. *It's the tree about which all others grow. See how the other trees swirl around it, like a snail shell, protecting it?* Mila turned carefully, following the spiral until the shape was lost. *In return, it protects us, makes sure the forest provides.*

Bjørn lives here, Oskar had said, reaching across to pinch Mila's arm.

Let's hope he's not hungry, teased Sanna, pinching her other arm.

Leave your little sister alone, said Papa with a sigh.

Mila had shuddered, looking about her. *But we take sap – doesn't that make him angry?*

We don't take more than we need, said Mama.

But Mila was not reassured. *Bjørn doesn't really kill anyone who hurts the heart tree – he's only a story, isn't he?*

Stories are just a different way of telling the truth, said Mama. *He'd only hurt people to protect the forest. Either way, the heart tree is precious. If it were harmed, the forest would die.*

And we'd have to leave, said Papa sadly, and Mila leant against his side. She had learnt her love for the forest from him.

But it won't happen, will it?

Of course not, said Mama gently.

And you'll never leave?

Mila had heard the smile in Papa's voice. *Never.*

He had, though, and, as if he had himself been the heart tree, winter stayed just as certainly as he'd gone, catching the forest in its cage of ice and snow. Mila hadn't climbed a tree since.

They were nearing the last of the traps, nearing the grove of birches that surrounded the heart tree. Mila could see them – thin silver spirits in the low winter light, shining against the dark bark of fir and larch. They seemed smaller than she remembered, and duller, though she supposed she was simply bigger. The coals beneath her skin hissed again. *Never harm the heart tree. Bjørn will get you.* Their father had repeated this so often it had hooked into their minds long before they'd been name-gifted.

Sanna saw they were close too, and clucked her tongue at the back of her throat, pulling on the reins to slow Dusha and Danya. They obeyed instantly and started a gentle walk, their breath flying up in great clouds.

Mila jumped from the sleigh to walk beside them, her hand on Dusha's high flank. She was warm even through Mila's glove, and Mila could feel the buzz of her breath, like a hive in the hollow trunk of a tree. Sanna stayed on the sleigh, shifting to the centre to balance it.

'*Stuta!*' Sanna lingered on the 's' sound between slightly parted teeth, like the whistle of their battered kettle, and the dogs stopped.

Mila did not. She passed beneath the final trap, a series of noose snares covered in a night's frost, laid at steady intervals along the frozen branches, hopeful of birds. Papa told them how once the whole forest was filled with wings. *Their song used to wake me! Can you imagine?*

Mila could never imagine.

One trap was laid low and Mila lifted it, finding the smear and body of a young shrike, barely bigger than a fledgling.

'Mila?' Sanna's voice was gentle.

'See how small it is?' murmured Mila over the muted rustle of the forest, the soft pant of the dogs. 'Only good for baiting.'

She crouched, legs sore from the sleigh, and prodded lightly at the bird. The feathers gave a little beneath her fingers. The bird was not frozen, which meant Oskar had not missed it from a previous visit. But it also meant he had not come to the traps today. He was not here.

'It's fresh?' asked Sanna.

Mila nodded, sharp tears gritting the corners of her eyes. She wiped them away impatiently and strode onwards, the final few strides that took her into the grove, to where she knew the heart tree grew. A tree that was taller and older than any other in the forest, stretching out its mighty branches until it seemed the whole sky was heart tree . . .

What she saw brought Mila to her knees.

Chapter Six

The Heart Tree

Behind her, Sanna gasped and even Pípa, who had never been here before, cried out.

'What's happened?'

The heart tree, once the tallest in the forest, ended at head-height, bark peeling off in great reams. The trunk lay at an angle, like a giant brought into a crashing slumber. It had been hacked across the roots, the wounds were stark and pulpy, its white insides shining, long-frozen sap dried and gleaming like honey mixed with freshly spilt blood. Ice had wormed inside and shattered the slices wider. There was no telling how long it had lain like this. Winter caught everything in slow time, even death. Around it, the other birches seemed to be leaning towards it, like mourners bowed by a burial pit.

The heart tree had been felled.

Mila's mind was racing. *Who has done this?* The sight sent fear and grief deep inside her bones. *Why?*

The stranger's cruel smile flashed into her head as a light hand rested on her fur-swathed back.

'Milenka—' started Sanna, but Mila flinched away as though her sister had struck her.

'Don't call me that,' she hissed, feeling the fear in her belly grow claws. 'I told you he'd been taken, and now we've wasted all this time, nearly a quarter-sun, when we should be going after them.'

Sanna's face drew in, shadows pinching under her high cheekbones. Her voice was still gentle when she spoke. 'I knew it was stupid to come, stupid to give you false hope—'

'You are the stupid one!' shouted Mila, making Danya whine and Pípa flinch. She kicked at a drift, sending powder flecking up her sister's thin face. 'Oskar hasn't gone, he's been taken!'

Sanna reached into her pouch and pulled out something glinting. 'The ring—'

Mila knocked her hand, sending the ring spinning into the snow. 'It means nothing!' she yelled. 'Oskar wouldn't leave!'

Pípa hesitantly stooped and picked the ring up from where it glimmered, like a drop of blood, in the white. 'Why do you have Oskar's ring?'

Neither sister answered her, eyes fixed on each other's

faces. Pípa was too young to remember that it had been Papa's before Oskar wore it. She slipped it on to her thumb.

'Careful, Pípa,' Mila said spitefully. 'You might leave too.'

Pípa frowned as the shadows in Sanna's face grew darker still. Their eldest sister narrowed her ice-blue eyes before turning away to the sleigh. 'We have to go. It tastes like snow.'

Mila felt it too, the clean cold under her tongue, the snap of the air around her exposed ear lobes, but she flushed hot with fury. She bent and picked up a handful of snow, throwing it hard at Sanna's back. It struck her squarely on the nape of her neck beneath her still-perfect bun, and slid down inside her cloak.

Sanna wheeled around, striding back to her, cloak swishing. She stopped so close Mila felt her breath, her fists clenched. Mila saw her anger matched in her sister's face.

'You think now is the time for a snow fight? You're acting like a baby, like Pípa—'

'Hey—' came their sister's retort.

'And you are acting like Papa!' screamed Mila.

Sanna's jaw clenched. 'What's that meant to mean?'

Mila swallowed the lump in her throat, willed the

tears back down. 'You've given up. You've given up on Oskar just as Papa gave up on us.'

'Milenka.' Sanna reached out again, and Mila flinched. 'Oskar's the one that's like Papa, not me.'

Mila stepped back, shaking her head. 'You didn't see him by the window. Someone was talking to him. Someone was scaring him.'

'It's true,' said Pípa. 'I saw him too.'

'Perhaps it was you who scared him, little mouse. You know how good you are at sneaking.' A faint smile tiptoed at the corners of Sanna's lips, but her eyes were sad. She held out her arms to Mila. 'You probably startled him while he was making plans to go.'

Mila let Sanna hold her. She felt suddenly very tired, limbs drooping like snow-weighted branches. She took a deep breath. Sanna smelt of the wood fire at home and the sharp tang of birch-tar soap. The same as Oskar did, when he'd hugged her last night. Mila cleared her throat, pushing gently away from her sister, and forced herself to look her in the eyes.

'I want to go to Stavgar.' She kept her voice deliberately calm. Shouting hadn't helped sway her sister – she had to try a different tack.

Sanna's dark eyebrows knitted. 'Why?'

'It's not far if we cut through from here,' said

Mila, pointing at the thinner trees to their right. 'The men said they were heading north, so they must've passed through Stavgar if they were taking the fastest route. If we . . .' Her voice trailed off as Sanna gave a loud tut.

'Mila, we are not going after him. If he didn't want to stay, then good riddance.'

Mila gritted her teeth. 'If they passed through Stavgar, we'll know whether Oskar was with them or not.'

As if she could hear the silent accusation, Sanna threw her hands up. 'Look, Mila. It's going to snow soon. If we go to Stavgar, we'll barely make it home before full-dark.'

'But we will if we go now.'

'I can't risk being out in the dark with Pípa—'

'I don't mind,' said Pípa eagerly. 'I like the dark.' Of all of them, she was in some ways the bravest.

'See,' urged Mila. 'Don't you want to be sure?'

'I'm already sure.' Sanna sighed. Mila stayed quiet. She could tell Sanna was thinking it over, or she'd have already turned the dogs for home. Finally, her sister nodded.

'Fine,' she said, on a great exasperated exhale.

Mila did not stop to savour the victory, only hurried to the sleigh, while Sanna led the dogs in a small semicircle to face north. She barely gave her sister time to secure her hold on the sleigh handle before snapping the reins.

'*Farash!*'

Chapter Seven

The Cord

The track to Stavgar was covered in deeper snow than the path to the heart tree, though the thick forest canopy had saved them from the worst of it. Before the endless winter it had been the main trading route, along which precious goods like wool, copper or ironwork came from the north, or salt, fish and fine cloth from the south. Now it was mainly used by the Oreksons, venturing to Stavgar for meat when the traps failed, or by Geir, visiting Sanna under the pretence of delivering knives.

Occasionally, when the snow eased a little, traders still passed by, so on these days if Sanna needed a new pot, or thread when gut would not do for mending, Oskar had to be roused at the crack of dawn. He was sent with furs to stand at the crossroads and wait. Despite the early start, Pípa and Mila would accompany him as often as they were allowed. Mila liked to see the outer boundaries of her forest, and wonder at the southern people, who sometimes had hair the colour of sunshine, even paler than Geir's, or the tall men who kept their beards plaited and beaded in a style she heard used to be all the rage in the north.

More precious than silk thread, or salt, was the gossip from the mountain city by the sea, where Mama had grown up. Bovnik had almost as many mines as Eldbjørn had trees, and it overlooked the Boreal Sea, where now the magical island of Thule was said to be caught in the ice, trapped by their eternal winter. The town was built so high up, Mama said, that, in the days before winter, the mountains pierced the sun at sunset and sent its light dripping down the pale buildings like egg yolk. Once it had been a thriving place, but they'd heard that since winter began the mines had become treacherous, and now it was all but abandoned.

It was at the trading crossroads, that Mila saw something in the snow. A faint glint, like grit in a wound.

'*Stuta!*'

She was not prepared for the sudden halt. The handle jabbed into her ribs as the dogs obeyed her, although Sanna had the reins, and Mila felt a stab of satisfaction at their loyalty.

Pípa tumbled sideways, and Sanna pitched forward,

nearly tipping over the handle. '*Javoyt!*' she shouted, rubbing her stomach. 'Are you trying to kill us?'

Mila wiped the smile from her face. 'I . . . I wanted . . .' But she'd lost the spot where she'd seen the glimmer. The snow shone a uniform greyish-white as she scanned it.

Sanna's face softened. 'The snow will have covered their tracks, Mila.'

Mila nodded. 'I'll just have a look.'

Sanna let out another sigh. 'Quickly, before I change my mind and turn us home.'

'As if the dogs would listen to you over me,' muttered Mila under her breath.

'What?'

'I'll be quick.'

Mila jumped off the sleigh and cast her eyes over the snow. It lay over the path like a sheet, ruching gently where tree roots lay.

'What're you looking for?' asked Pípa, but Mila only shrugged. Perhaps she had imagined it. Nothing seemed out of the ordinary, but as Mila turned back towards the sleigh she noticed a root had worked its way to the centre of the path. She scuffed her boot over it, but the it rolled under her foot. It was not a root at all.

Sanna was stamping her feet and tutting. 'Come *on*, Mila. Or I'm taking us home. Three . . . Sit down, Pípa!'

Mila ignored her. She bent down and brushed the snow aside. Something glinted against the white. She looked around quickly. Sanna was pointing to the seal-skin bed, where Pípa was standing up, her other hand on the reins.

'Two . . .'

Gold cord. It was a piece of the gold cord the stranger had worn around his boots – the same cord all his men had worn. Mila hesitated. She didn't really want to touch it, even with gloves.

'One! That's it, we're going home.'

'No, I'm coming.' Mila picked up the cord and put it in her cloak before she could think better of it. Her heart thrummed.

This time it was Mila who was caught unawares when Sanna shouted, '*Farash!*' Her sister's sly grin as she scrambled to grab hold made her glad she had not shown Sanna what she'd found. She would dismiss the gold cord as nothing, but Mila could feel it was important.

Sanna thought she knew best, thought she knew their brother, thought he thought like her. Mila looked ahead at the running dogs, and beyond, into the winter-caught forest. Soon they would be in Stavgar, and Sanna would know the truth – that Oskar was nothing like her, or Papa, and everything like Mila.

*

Snowflakes dappled Mila's face just as Stavgar began to reveal itself, signs of civilization coming slow as a thaw through the trees. It had been a year at least since Mila had visited, and little seemed to have changed. A couple of livestock pens dotted the route, with low-slung turf outhouses.

Sanna slowed the dogs to a walk, and jumped down to stretch her legs. Mila did the same, to spare the dogs. The path was cleared of snow, but they had run for hours now without a rest. Mila ran her hand along Danya's back, feeling the slick nubs of spine.

'They're tired,' she said.

'Did you bring food?' asked Sanna, and Mila remembered the dried elk strips she'd packed into her cloak. She pulled out a handful and passed some to Pípa and Sanna before holding one in each palm and letting the dogs chomp them down. She tasted one herself, the tough saltiness comforting, as she glanced around the low banks edging the road. A prickle of fear crept up the back of her neck.

'Sanna?'

'Mm?' She had her mouth full.

'Look where we are.'

Sanna looked. Mila watched her stop chewing, her

cold-flushed cheeks paling. Immediately she took up the reins and nodded for Mila to get on the bed beside Pípa.

'What is it?' Pípa asked, peering around, and Mila felt her little sister's sharp inhale of breath. Crouched in a turn of the path was a building, so overgrown it seemed more forest than house. It slunk low to the ground, like a beast stalking prey, turf roof sagging in the centre, bowed by bare vines that muscled up like thorns.

'Is that . . . the mage's house?' Pípa whispered as Sanna ordered the dogs on.

Mila nodded. She had never seen him herself, only heard stories from Geir, but it was enough to make her cross her fingers against dark magic. Pípa's cloak pocket bulged, and she knew her sister had done the same. They rounded a bend and the house slid out of sight.

'Do you think he saw us? Can he put the eye on us?'

'Hush, Pípa.' Mila put her arm around her little sister. 'It's only stories.'

Just a different way of telling the truth. Her mother's words rose unbidden, and she pushed them away, sent them spinning from her in a puff of cold breath.

Chapter Eight

Stavgar

More dwellings began to line the road, and at last they reached the square, where the jarl and other wealthy villagers lived in houses with richly carved lintels and stone-slab roofs. One whole side of the square was taken up with the meethouse, a huge structure with wooden pillars striping its side.

'They sound like they're celebrating,' said Sanna, and Mila heard raised voices coming from within. Now they were here, her dread for Oskar returned in full force. What if no one had seen the man and boys pass by? Or worse, what if they had?

The square was swept clear of snow and gravel gritted the icy ground, making it easier to walk but harder to sleigh. The sisters clambered off, Mila's legs stiff and complaining as blood rushed back into them, and Sanna tied up the dogs at a long trough opposite the meethouse.

Dusha attempted to lick the frozen water, snuffling

plaintively as her tongue rasped on the ice.

'Stop, you silly goose,' said Mila, cracking it with her elbow so the dogs could drink the water beneath the icy pane. She placed her hand on Dusha's ruff, the ground swaying around her. Soon they would know the truth of it. Sanna seemed so sure. *So I must be sure, too.*

Mila squared her shoulders and followed her sisters to the meethouse door: a massive, whorled slab of oak with an iron ring for a handle. Sanna had stopped short, and Mila saw that she was pinching her already-flushed cheeks and checking her brooch was straight.

'Really, Sanna?' Mila's lip curled in disgust. 'You're worried about Geir seeing you?'

She pushed past her sister without waiting for an answer, feeling the cold of the metal even through her fur-lined glove as she heaved the door open.

The enormous fire at the centre of the room was blazing, flames leaping higher than the heads of the people crowding around it. The wall of heat hit Mila's frozen face, bringing the blood tingling to her cheeks, and she pulled off her hat as her scalp began to itch with sweat.

It was only when she looked up from stowing it in her pocket that she realized the room had fallen silent, and that every face was turned towards her. The man nearest her called, 'The Orekson girls!' and the room broke into noise again.

Mila pulled on his arm. 'Excuse me, I was wondering if—'

But at that moment, the meeting bell was struck. A low, sonorous ripple spread around the walls, followed by silence. Mila looked at the speaking platform, a raised jut of wood reached by steps struck into the loam wall.

A woman in a green cloak stood there, her hand on the bell's tongue. Mila recognized her broad, handsome face. Bretta, the town's jarl.

'Enough bickering,' she said, in a voice as low as the bell's. 'I will listen to petitions one at a time, but, to save tedious details, here are the facts I think we all share. At dawn, fourteen men rode into our square—'

'Fourteen,' hissed Mila to Sanna, who had moved to stand beside her, Pípa at her other side. 'There were thirteen that came to our home. Oskar must be with them.'

'Shhh!' snapped Sanna. 'I'm listening.'

'They wished to trade for supplies for their journey north. As is customary, we invited them in here, and sent for the men to welcome them to our town.'

'And boys,' wailed a pitiful voice. Mila craned her neck and saw a copper-haired woman, face twisted and tear-stained. 'My boy Geir has gone.'

56

'Oh, Sanna!' Pípa raised her hand to her mouth, and Mila looked sharply at her sister. Sanna swayed, grasping Geir's brooch. Mila took Sanna's other hand, and squeezed it tightly.

'Your son is seventeen and so nearly a man,' snapped Bretta. 'He is responsible for his own foolish choices. I myself met with their leader.' She gave a nearly imperceptible shudder. 'And he told us of their journey. The riches they had seen, and were to return to . . . He claimed to have more treasure at his home, greater than any other.'

Her voice sounded wistful. 'It sounded like fantasy to me, especially coming from such a ragged bunch, and I thought the boys saw through them just as I did. I was wrong. They are gone, all of them.'

'Was my brother among them?'

Sanna's voice made Mila start and pull her sweating hand away.

'Who spoke?' said Bretta sharply, and the crowd parted like wheat beneath a scythe.

Sanna stepped forward to stand beside the fire. It lit her black hair a shimmering blue. Mila felt rooted to the spot.

'I have come from the south forest. I'm Yelfer Orekson's eldest daughter.'

'Ah, yes,' said Bretta. Her tone was instantly disapproving. Their father's betrayal was well known here in Stavgar. 'And your question?'

'Was my brother with them? Oskar.' Sanna's voice shook. Mila felt a rush of sympathy and pride – Geir being gone was another shock, but her sister stood strong.

Bretta regarded her keenly. 'I could not say. His companions were hooded. Is your brother gone too?'

'Yes.'

'Selfish boy,' said Bretta bitterly. 'Aren't you only sisters without him?'

Sanna nodded. 'So they – the boys – they weren't taken? Or forced to go?'

Bretta shook her head, and Mila felt as though she stood on a precipice. Her head wheeled. It could not be true.

'They went chasing treasure,' Bretta said with contempt. 'It seems it is always a man's lot to leave, a woman's duty to be left.'

The men in the room shifted uncomfortably under Bretta's sharp gaze.

'I wouldn't be so certain if I were you.' A new voice, light and almost sing-song, came from a dark corner beside the oak door.

The room seemed to move as one animal, shrinking back, as a short, cloaked shape stepped forward into the firelight's reach. The man beside Mila spat, and she saw his wife cross her fingers. A chill, fine as a cobweb, seemed to fall across them all, as a boy stepped into the light.

Chapter Nine

The Mage

He was barely taller than Mila, and not much older. His fine blond-white hair settled like a cloud about his shoulders, his tatty robes of dark blue a little long. Mila could not help but recoil when he looked up. His eyes were pale as moonstones.

'Is he blind?' she heard Pípa whisper to Sanna.

Though she had spoken so quietly that Mila had barely heard, his eyes flicked to Pípa, and he shook his head. The web-like chill cracked into scuttling spiders of fear across Mila's neck.

'You were asked not to come,' said Bretta. Even the indomitable jarl seemed nervous of him. 'We told you to stay away.'

'I have something to say, if you would hear it.' The voice was whisper light, but commanding. 'I said it would happen. I said it was only a matter of time until he came.'

Bretta held a hand up. 'Please, Rune. We don't need a story now.'

Rune . . .

This boy was the much-feared mage of Stavgar? She'd always imagined him as imposing as an oak, but here he was, not more than a couple of years between them.

Rune smiled, showing gappy teeth. 'Who said anything about a story? He came, you saw him. You spoke with him.'

'I speak with many people,' said Bretta, her tone making it clear her patience would not hold much longer. 'If you have something to say, say it, simply and fast.'

'They did not go willingly.' Rune had turned to Sanna, who flinched. 'The Bear took them.'

The pennant fluttered in Mila's mind – a bear beneath a tree rooted in gold. She slipped her hand inside her pocket, gripped the cord. It felt strangely warm and she let go.

'I saw no bear,' said Bretta.

'He keeps himself hidden,' said Rune, still staring at Sanna. Mila drew closer to her sisters, and Rune's eyes moved to her. 'It takes a special kind of person to see.'

'Enough!' Bretta snapped, and Mila jumped. 'I saw no bear, I saw no struggle. I saw only boy after boy chasing adventure at the cost of family.'

Mila suddenly did not want to hear it – any of it. She wanted to be with the dogs, at home, with Pípa and Oskar and—

She gave a great sob – 'Sanna,' she gasped – and fell to the reed-strewn floor, her legs and chest aching. Sanna and Pípa knelt down beside her, and the jarl joined them.

Mila blinked, trying to clear her hazy head. The jarl was even more impressive up close, her nose straight as an arrow, her thick brown eyebrows like fletches, her eyes grey flint.

Bretta considered them a moment. 'You can't stay in the forest alone. You can stay in my home. Go there now.' She raised her hand and her voice so the whole room could all hear her: 'We will weather this together.'

'Thank you,' said Sanna, bowing her head.

Bretta turned back to the hall, and, considering themselves dismissed, Sanna began to help Mila to her feet. Mila felt herself about to fall again, but a bony hand, surprisingly strong, supported her under her armpit.

'You saw,' said the sing-song voice.

'What are you doing?' said Sanna harshly, pulling Mila away from Rune.

Mila met the milky eyes, and it seemed as though Rune spoke directly inside her head. 'You'll find me in the first house.'

It was only Sanna's reply that made Mila feel Rune had spoken aloud at all: 'She'll not be coming to your house, nor speaking to you. Leave us alone.'

Mila felt numb even before Pípa opened the door. It had stopped snowing, and Dusha and Danya were chomping on the icicles that hung from the side of the trough, lips pulled back from their teeth. Normally their daftness would make Mila smile, but now she felt a hollowness like she never had before. Not after Mama. Not even after Papa.

'That's the jarl's house, isn't it?' Pípa was pointing at the second-largest building in the square: a sturdy, stone-walled house with a door painted blood-red. They knocked and a servant opened it, standing aside once Sanna had explained why they were there.

Mila let Sanna guide her into the jarl's house. She felt thick furs under her booted feet, and the warmth of the fire as Sanna placed her gently before it. Pípa crept to Mila's side and began fiddling with Papa's ring, which was still on her thumb. It made Mila sick to look at it.

'You think we should stay?' Pípa asked.

Sanna sighed. 'It seems sensible.'

'What if Oskar comes back? He won't know where we are.'

Sanna clenched her eyes shut in a way that told Mila she did not think he would ever come back. Her hand toyed with Geir's brooch, still pinned to her cloak.

'If Oskar returns from the north, he will pass through Stavgar anyway,' she said at last. 'We can decide what to do then. It's only a quarter-sun sleigh home after all.'

There fell an unsteady silence, and Mila realized Sanna was going to say nothing of the boy with the moonstone eyes.

'What about the mage?' she asked.

'Yes, was that him?' Pípa said, digging a sharp elbow into Mila's side to hoist herself more upright. 'Are mages the same as witches?'

'Witches aren't real,' snapped Sanna. 'They're mad, people who believe themselves magic. They have some knowledge of herbs, and I heard Rune's mother was respected by some in her day.' Her wrinkled nose showed she was not among them. 'But Geir . . .' Sanna looked at her lap, and Mila saw the glint of tears in her eyes. 'Geir said he's little more than a lunatic. Whatever Rune told you, forget it.'

'He's only a boy,' said Mila, shuddering. 'I thought—'

'Unnatural beast,' hissed Sanna, but Mila could sense fear under her sister's disgust. 'Why didn't he go, too?'

They fell silent. Oskar and Geir's absence seemed to

swell to fill the gap. At long last, Sanna stretched wearily, and yawned.

'Bed now, I think.'

They all climbed into their furs, and Mila's heavy body dragged her down, down, sleep covering her as fully as snow over tracks.

Chapter Ten

The First House

ind me in the first house.

F Mila's dreams had been full of the mage's words, and she woke knowing what she must do. Sanna and Pípa were still sleeping when she sneaked out. First she went to the dogs, to check they were settled into the kennels. It would have been quicker to sleigh, but Dusha and Danya were excitable, leaping up to lick her face and barking. Mila knew they'd make a racket if she harnessed them outside.

She looked over her shoulder. No one was following, and no faces looked out from the ice windows of the turf houses. She lengthened her stride. Only yesterday they had hurried away from the mage's house, crossed their fingers against it. And now here she was, hurrying towards it.

Besides, her legs had lost their aching and were filled with a restless, twitching energy. She hoped the walk might tire them. Her stomach felt filled with moths, darting around a bright point of hope that Rune might be able to tell her something about Oskar.

Either side, the trees leant in and whispered. She wished they could speak, wished they could tell her what they'd seen the night Oskar left. *Was taken*, she corrected herself, though Bretta had seemed certain they had gone willingly. The jarl was the sort of person whose opinion felt like fact.

Mila thrust her hands into her cloak pockets, and instantly pulled her right hand back out. It felt as though she had grasped an icicle. She'd forgotten about the cord. Bile rose in her throat when she saw it was no longer gold and pliable, but as twisted and dark as a dried root. It sat rigid in her hand, emanating that vicious cold, as if it were a living thing that had been plucked, and was now shrivelled and dead.

Mila shuddered, but she did not throw it away. Instinct had led her to find it, and instinct told her to keep it. She put it back in her pocket, and continued walking, keeping her right hand warm in her left armpit. She didn't want to touch the cord again.

Finally, the bank to her left rose, and the turf roof of the mage's house peeked over the top. It still felt to Mila that the house was poised, ready to move, like in the story

Papa had told her about the witch whose house had hen's legs. As Mila drew closer she heard singing, misty as a chill morning. She scrambled up the bank, boots skidding on black ice, and listened.

At home you sleep
At home you're safe
Until a face
At the window calls

Heart pounding, she moved to the iceless window, the cold nipping her ears as she lifted her hat to hear better.

It knows your fears
And if it knows your name
You can't turn your face
From the winter's call.

The singing stopped. A moment later, the unpainted door opened. 'Winter-well-met, Mila.'

Sanna might believe witches only existed in stories, but Mila felt as though she were in a fairy tale now, one that would not end well for the child about to enter a stranger's house, even if the stranger were a child too. Mila saw now that his eyes were not completely white from pupil to lid. It only seemed that way, because his irises were the palest grey-blue, like river ice. He was perhaps only half a hand taller than she, and his blond-white hair was neatly combed now, less a cloud and more a river.

Mila took a deep breath, and stepped inside.

'Welcome,' said Rune. 'Shoes off.'

Mila unlaced her boots and placed them by the door, accepting the soft felt slippers Rune held out.

There was just one room, and the house felt even smaller than it looked from the outside, because it was so full of things. Glass vials – real glass! – of all sizes were scattered haphazardly over every surface – the dark wood table, bench and fur-strewn bed. Bunches of herbs swayed from beams that shuddered when Rune closed the door behind Mila.

A fire hissed and spat in the back corner of the room, and above it, set into the wall, was another grate that filtered the flames and left only smoke rising to the chimney. It was the palest white, like wisps of mist, and smelt of apples.

Above the smoke hung several slabs of fish. From their pink flesh and size Mila guessed they were salmon, but only the richest could afford salmon. She had tried it only once, a petal-thin, rose-coloured wafer that Mama had served one spring solstice, accompanied by heart tree sap sweet and golden as honey.

'Don't mind the mess,' said Rune, expertly picking his way to a chair beside the fire. 'I'm not used to visitors.

Come. Sit.'

Mila followed his path to the fire, trying to stop her cloak catching on the objects she had no name for on the ground.

'Ouch!' She stepped on something small and hard, and lifted her foot to see two bone dice inscribed with symbols.

'Sorry,' said Rune, with a sudden bark of laughter that made his face look as young as Pípa's. He held out his hand for them. 'I was scrying.' He threw the dice straight in the fire.

'Oh!' said Mila. 'Did I break them?'

'No, no. I just need to renew them. You'll have confused the runes – they aren't used to feet.'

Mila stared at him. 'Do you . . . live here alone?' She looked around at the clutter. 'No grown-ups?'

'I'm quite grown-up enough, thank you,' said Rune, not unkindly. 'Besides, would a grown-up let you do this?'

He reached into the fire with his bare hand, and even as Mila cried out for him to be careful, he fished out two smoking dice and placed them on the fur hearthrug. They began to smoulder and Rune batted them with his sleeve a couple of times.

'I am so glad you came, and so soon,' he said distractedly. 'Because there is very little time, and I am only

allowed to ask you twice.'

Mila blinked away from the dice and the singed fur, and focused again on the strange boy. 'Ask me twice?'

'To come. Otherwise it means you do not want to be here. And if you do not want to be here, it means you are not willing. And if you are not willing—'

'Willing?' said Mila, looking around nervously. What if Rune wanted her to participate in scrying, or some other dark art that Sanna definitely wouldn't approve of? Not that she would approve of anything Mila was currently doing, or seeing.

'If you are not willing,' continued Rune gently, 'you do not have the heart for it.'

'Heart for what?'

'For what I am about to tell you,' said Rune slowly, as though Mila were Pípa's age. He reached for a glass bottle of amber liquid and unstoppered it. Mila smelt something strong and sweet. 'Do you want some mead? I find it strengthens the heart.'

'I'm twelve,' said Mila. 'How old are you?

'It's not strong.' Rune shrugged and swigged.

Mila raised her eyebrow the way Sanna had taught her.

Rune made a *pfft* sound, blowing air from his lips. 'Milk, then? I have fresh from my goat.'

Mila felt she was the wrong age for milk too, but she

nodded, and Rune manoeuvred his way to the opposite corner, beside the back door. With a flourish, he removed a woollen blanket from a large black goat. Mila raised a hand to her mouth, startled, and Rune held a copper pan under the goat's udder.

'Come on, Lunka, be nice.'

The goat bleated once, then went back to chewing the straw laid before her. Once the pan was filled, Rune threw the wool back over the goat, and returned to the fire, suspending the pan from two hooks over the flames.

'Be ready in a minute,' said the boy, as though having a goat covered with a blanket in your house was the most ordinary thing in the world.

Mila gaped, wondering again if she had made the right decision to come.

'Now,' said Rune, taking another swig of mead. 'We may as well get started. As I said, there's not much time left.'

'Time left before what?'

'Before you lose your brother for ever.'

Chapter Eleven

A Between Place

Mila felt a thump in her chest, as if her heart were reminding her to breathe. 'What do you mean? Do you know where he is?'

'You saw, you see. You knew your brother hadn't gone of his own accord, that—'

'He had been taken.' Mila finished the sentence with him.

Rune nodded. 'Just like all the others. Taken by the Bear.'

'The stranger?' said Mila. 'That's his name?'

'It's the name others gave him,' said Rune. 'You'll have heard his story, no doubt, but perhaps you know it by another name. Bjørn, the guardian of the forest. What do you know about him?'

'That he is a bear, and he lives in the . . .' She hesitated, the horrible vision of the birch grove ghosting into her mind. 'In the heart tree, and protects the forest.'

'Protects the forest, yes,' said Rune thoughtfully. 'At all costs.'

Mila shuddered, remembering the destroyed heart tree. 'What does that mean?'

'That he'll destroy anything that harms it,' said Rune. 'And people do tend to harm things, don't we?'

Here comes mighty Bjørn, planting human hearts like corn, chorused Mila's mind unhelpfully, before she could stop it.

Rune sang again.

It knows your fears
And if it knows your name
You can't turn your face
From the winter's call.

'If it – he – knows your name . . .' Mila faltered.

'He can call you,' said Rune. 'Control you. People give their names away too easy. They don't understand there's sense in the old traditions, in naming your children falsely until the evil eye passes over. Do you have your true name?'

Mila nodded.

'Shame. It's easier if you don't know it. Then it's harder for him to find it. You must keep it hidden from him, or else there would be no point in helping you follow.'

Mila was about to tell him Bjørn had already found it: that Oskar had given it to him in the clearing at home. But the mage was saying Mila would not be able to go if the Bear knew her name. She swallowed the sentence down and instead asked, 'Follow where?'

'North.'

'Yes,' said Mila impatiently. Rune's roundabout way of talking might suit stories or songs, but it was very annoying. 'But where north? Where has he taken my brother? And the others?'

'To Thule.'

Mila sat back in her chair. She could believe that a threatening stranger had managed to kidnap her brother; believe, having seen the size of him, that he was called the Bear; but now she was being told that he lived on Thule – the magical island trapped by winter. It was nonsense.

'I can see what you're thinking.' Rune's gaze was suddenly focused and sharp, as it had been on Sanna in the meethouse. 'That Thule is a fairy tale. But if you go back far enough, fairies lived to tell their own tales. Some of us understand that impossible places are possible.'

'But Thule isn't a real place,' said Mila, exasperated.

Rune placed his thin hands one over the other. 'There are many realms, Mila, seen and unseen. They overlap a bit like fish scales. Sometimes, they intertwine.' He laced his fingers.

'But no one's ever been there.'

'That's where you're wrong. Plenty go . . . are taken . . .' Rune's gaze went far away, as though he stood on a hill-top. 'But very few return.'

Mila frowned, remembering what Sanna had said. 'Why weren't you taken?'

'I'm a mage, Mila. I have ways to protect myself.'

'But not the others?' Mila's anger flared hot as flame.

Rune sat back suddenly in his chair, as though Mila had pushed him. 'I tried to warn them!' His voice was full of hurt, almost sulky. 'But you saw how they talk to me. Bretta has never liked me. They treat me like a diseased animal, or else like a mad child.'

'But why?' cried Mila. 'Why does he take them?'

Rune relented and leant forward, firelight spreading over his thin lips, narrow nose, his huge moonstone eyes. He seemed to Mila at once as young as Pípa and as ancient as a tree.

'Because he wants us gone from the forest, Mila. He wants us *dead*. That's why he sent the winter, and took spring to Thule for himself, that's why he takes the boys—'

'*He* sent the winter?' Mila gasped. Rune sat back and nodded gravely. 'Why?'

'Now that is a true mystery,' said Rune. 'I have my theories, though.'

'Tell me,' said Mila.

Rune stared into the fire. 'We have to find a way past winter.'

'What is that supposed to mean?' Mila had had enough. She threw up her hands and made to stand, but Rune held out a pacifying palm.

'I know you feel what I say does not make sense, Mila, but does it make more sense than what your sister believes happened – that your brother left you?'

Mila felt a thin thread in her chest break, the thread that had held together her belief in her sister.

'No,' she said, simply.

The boy smiled. 'I knew you saw. You care, Mila, deeply, and that makes you pay attention. It also makes you similar to the Bear, in a way—'

'I'm nothing like him!'

'You're fierce,' continued Rune. 'You'll do anything to protect what you love, I can see that in you. And that makes you dangerous to him. There are things in the world that you have to look at with more than your eyes, hear with more than your ears, touch with more than your fingers. And you can do that, you have shown that by coming here, by realizing the Bear was more and worse than a man. That means you can bring your brother back.'

Hope must have shown in Mila's face because Rune continued solemnly, 'But you do know, if you want him back, it won't be easy? It will be the opposite of easy. It is a dangerous journey to Thule. And you don't have much time.'

The air no longer smelt of apples, but of burnt milk.

'How do you know all this?' Mila said, her voice barely above a whisper.

Rune turned his face full to the fire. 'I'm a mage, Mila. I can read patterns, sense truths. I know most fear me, even despise me for it. But it is just what I am.' He turned his strange eyes upon her. 'We must leave for Thule tonight, if you want your brother back. And we cannot tell anyone where we are going. They will only try to stop us.'

'We? You're coming too?' Mila felt something a little like relief, though she was not sure Sanna would approve of her going on the journey with the mage; then again, Sanna would not approve of her going at all.

'I always meant to.'

Mila hesitated. Did she really believe what Rune had told her? An immortal named the Bear, causing an ever-lasting winter, coming to take boys. A magical island.

Wasn't it simpler to believe that Oskar had tired of their life and gone seeking riches?

Simpler, and harder.

She felt she should ask for some sort of proof of all the impossible things the mage had told her. But hadn't she felt something was different – dangerous, *difficult* – the moment she'd seen the stranger? His silencing of the dogs, his feet atop the snow, bound in gold, his sudden sinking down.

'I found something,' she said, pulling the cord from her cloak. 'But it wasn't like this when I got it. It was . . .'

She trailed off, because Rune was looking at the cord with triumph flashing across his face.

'I told you,' he said in a hoarse voice. 'I said you could see.'

Mila held it out, but Rune drew back, shaking his head. 'No, no. You must keep it. Bring this, and something of your brother's, something he wore and loved.'

'I have his hunting knife.' She pulled it from her belt to show him.

'Good,' said Rune. 'Do you suppose your family can spare a dog and sleigh?'

'Dusha will be able to manage us both,' said Mila. 'If we don't bring much.'

'We don't need much. Leave me in charge of food and

supplies,' he added, suddenly practical, 'and meet me at the top crossroads at high moon.'

He rose, and Mila did too, her blood pounding as she crossed the cluttered room to pull on her boots.

'And, Mila?'

She paused in the doorway, the cold biting her cheeks.

'Don't let anyone see you leave. There can be no delays.'

Mila nodded, and the door was closed behind her. She scuttered over the bank and back to the road. Her breath was as loud as a westerly wind in her ears. *I'm going*, she thought, to make it real. *I'm going to save Oskar.*

Chapter Twelve

Lies

It had taken Mila's best lying face to convince Sanna she had not been at the mage's house.

'Where were you, then? You weren't with the dogs, I checked.'

'I was . . .' Mila thought quickly, 'climbing.'

Sanna narrowed her eyes suspiciously. 'Climbing? You haven't done that since . . .'

Papa left passed silently between them. Mila nodded, insides wrenching with guilt as Sanna's face softened. She knew her sister was mourning not just Oskar but Geir as well.

I'm lying for them, she reminded herself. *So I can help Oskar.*

They passed the day quietly, Sanna compulsively sweeping their spotless room, Pípa and Mila playing games beside the fire. Mila was just beginning to lose hope that she would have a chance to make an inconspicuous exit, when there came a knock on the door.

'Winter-well-met,' said Bretta, striding in without waiting for them to answer. Mila supposed it was her house, but she could not help but feel a spike of dislike for the jarl. She seemed so pleased with herself. 'I've come to ask you to join us in the meethouse for dinner.'

Sanna almost bowed and said, 'Thank you, Jarl Bretta.'

Pípa caught Mila's gaze and rolled her eyes.

'Wonderful,' said Bretta grandly, and looked them all over. 'There are fresh clothes in the chest.'

She strode out again, leaving the door wide open. Mila got up and closed it as Sanna started fussing over her reflection in the ice window.

'I look a mess! Mila, fetch me something, would you?'

Mila heaved open the oak lid of the chest and found fine woollen dresses of green and grey. She pulled out a green one with yellow stitching and passed it to Sanna.

'Aren't you two changing?' said Sanna, fussing with her hair.

'I need to wash,' said Mila, indicating the jug and basin in the corner. 'Why don't you go ahead? I don't want you to miss any of the feast.'

'Pípa needs a wash too,' said Sanna decidedly. 'You two hurry up, though.'

Sanna looked almost happy as she threw on her cloak and left the room.

Pípa slid off her perch by the fire and went to tug on Mila's hand. 'She doesn't seem too sad about being here, does she?'

'She's just looking forward to a feast,' said Mila, something in her chest softening as she crouched beside her youngest sister. 'She's hungry. I am too. I'm mostly sad, though.'

'Me too,' said Pípa, her wide brown eyes looking around the chamber. 'I want to be at home. I want Oskar to be there too.'

'Píp?' In that moment Mila longed to tell Pípa. But she knew her sister would cry, and insist she didn't go. She'd tell Sanna, and then they'd never get Oskar back.

'I don't feel like washing any more. We can just say we did.'

'Good,' said Pípa, who hated being clean.

'Do you want me to plait your hair?'

'Yes,' said Pípa decisively, plonking herself down on the bearskin. 'But not so tight as Sanna does it.'

'Don't you enjoy your scalp being lifted off your skull?' teased Mila, and Pípa twisted around and crumpled her little face in a look of disgust. 'I'll be gentle.'

She combed her fingers through Pípa's hair. It was

threaded with auburn, like her own and Mama's, but had Sanna's soft straightness – Mila had always envied her that. Mila felt a plunging in her stomach. Her going would be hardest of all on Pípa. She was quiet on the rare occasions they came into contact with other children, and she had a tendency to stare, which even Mila found unsettling sometimes. Sanna had less and less time for her.

She cleared her throat and said, 'Do you like it here, Píp?'

Pípa's thin shoulders shrugged. 'I'd rather be home. I wish things were like normal.'

'With us arguing over a cabbage?'

Pípa giggled. 'With us, and Sanna not so mean, and Oskar . . .' her high voice went higher still. 'Here. Or there. Oskar home. Mila . . . it's not my fault, is it?'

Mila stopped untangling. 'What do you mean?'

'Well, Papa going was my fault, wasn't it?'

Mila reached her arms around her little sister and pulled her on to her lap so she could look down into her worried face. Pípa's lip was wobbling.

'Why do you say that?'

'Because Mama died having me.' Pípa's eyes were bright. 'And Papa left because Mama—'

'It's not your fault. Mama was sick before she had

you,' said Mila fiercely, squeezing Pípa so tight she squirmed. 'None of this is your fault.' She pushed her gently upright, keeping her tone brisk even as she blinked away tears.

'Promise?'

'Promise.' She sectioned Pípa's hair into three and smoothed it over her shoulders and back. It fell to the floor, pooling in Mila's lap. A few slow moments passed. 'What do you think happened, Píp? To Oskar.'

Pípa held her breath in the way she always did when she was thinking hard. She held it so long Mila wondered how she didn't faint or go red. It was like she was dead. Finally, the breath came gushing out as she said, 'I don't think Sanna and Bretta are right.'

'You don't think he would go?'

'No,' said Pípa in such a decisive voice it made Mila's heart swell. 'I don't think he would leave us. Maybe Sanna, because she's so grumpy. But you and me and the dogs? He loves us.'

Papa loved us too. It didn't stop him.

'How much longer?' said Pípa impatiently. 'My neck is aching.'

'It's because you slouch,' said Mila, taking up the sections of hair and beginning to braid.

Pípa sat up straighter, and Mila could see the ring

glinting on her thumb as she toyed with it. They sat quietly a moment, Mila looping strand over strand.

'You think so too, don't you?'

'Think what?' said Mila.

'He didn't want to go.'

'No,' said Mila, trying to sound as decisive as her little sister. 'I don't think he did.'

'What are we going to do about it?'

Mila's fingers turned all thumbs, and she dropped the centre section. 'If there was something to be done, would you do it? If you were older, I mean.'

'Of course. And why would I have to be older?' said Pípa, her voice frowny. 'The grown-ups aren't doing anything.'

Mila's heart was beating very fast. Of course she couldn't tell Pípa. Whatever she thought, she *was* too young to go with them on what was sure to be a dangerous journey. And Rune had told her not to say anything to anyone. She finished braiding and held her hand out over Pípa's shoulder. Pípa handed her two bone pins and Mila slid them crosswise to hold the plait in place.

Pípa spun around on her knees, braid whipping around so Mila had to lean back. 'Careful!'

'You're not going too?' Pípa's dark eyes were wide. She leant forward so Mila could feel her hot breath, small hands pressing hard on Mila's shoulders. 'You'd tell me?'

'Yes,' Mila lied, trying not to blink or fidget or do any of the things that would give away the truth. Pípa looked deep into Mila's eyes, her face so serious she looked far older than her seven years of winter. Mila almost laughed. Finally Pípa sat back.

'All right.' She jumped to her feet. 'Shall we go and find Sanna? I'm hungry.'

'You know what, Píp? I think I do need that wash after all,' said Mila, fetching her sister's cloak from its hook.

'But you said—'

'I know,' said Mila briskly, fastening it under Pípa's chin. 'But I feel all grimy. You go to the meethouse. I'll follow.'

Pípa sighed like Sanna. 'All right.'

She left without a backwards glance, and Mila held her arms stiffly by her sides to keep from running after her and hugging her tight.

'Goodbye, Píp,' she whispered.

Chapter Thirteen

High Moon

The lie souring in her stomach, Mila took one last look around the room, then hurried out into the night.

The path to the dog shed took her past the square, and she hugged the shadows. She could hear voices coming from the meethouse, and as she stood shivering, waiting for a moment when she could cross the square unseen, she imagined her family inside, warm and fed.

Mila felt such a pull of love it made her belly ache – though that may have been partly hunger. She should have gone for an early dinner. It suddenly all felt impossible and silly.

Since Papa left, Mila had spent her days thinking things through. Overthinking. She no longer delighted in climbing trees, like Pípa, or plunging into icy rivers, like Sanna. She was content to watch, listening to stories of other people's adventures, and she knew that

88

adventurers were nothing like her.

They were not afraid of heights or cold, fast-flowing water. Sanna would be a far better rescuer. Even Pípa had stronger nerves. But Mila was the one going. And perhaps that was enough: to be the one who believed. What had Rune said? The one who *saw*. She had seen what no one else had – she had seen the Bear first, had seen him hover on the snow, had seen Oskar talking to him through the ice window.

And while she thought about it, wasn't she being brave right now? She ducked her head and ran full pelt across the square, hoping no one was watching from the high, small windows. She reached the kennel and pulled the door open.

There were perhaps twelve dogs in the cramped space, and when she slipped in they surged towards her, leaping and whining. Dusha pushed forward and made high-pitched sounds, leaping to lick her face.

'All right, Dusha,' she murmured. 'Hush now, hush.'

The other dogs quietened when they realized she had not brought food. Mila ran a comforting hand over Danya, who looked unimpressed by the other dogs' lack of restraint. She lowered her face to his ruff and hugged him close. 'Be good.'

'What are you doing?'

The voice was quiet but Mila jumped as though it had shouted. She had not heard the door open, and she turned quickly. Pípa was there, her thin face pale and all angles in the moonlight, her arms heaped with bread. Mila's heart sank.

'Píp, I'm—'

'Are you going somewhere?' Pípa eyed the harness in her hands, which Mila tried to hide behind her.

'No, I'm not—'

'You said you wouldn't go!' Pípa's voice rose tremulously, and Mila hurried to shush her. 'If Sanna hadn't sent me with food for the dogs, you would have gone without me! You lied.'

'I couldn't tell you,' said Mila desperately. 'Please, Pípa, don't tell anyone.'

'I won't,' said Pípa determinedly. 'Because I'm going with you.'

'No.'

'Yes,' said Pípa. 'Or I'll scream.'

She took a deep breath and held it. Mila felt as if she were about to scream herself. 'You can't come with me. It's going to be dangerous—'

'You're going after Oskar.' It was not a question, but Mila nodded anyway. 'He's my brother too. And you're my sister. You have to take me with you.'

Pípa dropped the bread and the dogs surged forward again, chomping on the black loaves. Pípa pulled the harness from Mila's hands, but Mila held tight.

'I can't take you, Píp. You're too little—'

'I'm tall for my age,' snapped Pípa.

Mila tried to think as she wrestled the harness free of Pípa's grip and led Dusha outside to where their sleigh sat beside several others. She pulled back the sealskin covering and Pípa immediately sat on it.

'The load's too big for Dusha,' snapped Mila. 'You're making me late.'

'Late for who?'

Mila said nothing.

'You're not going without me,' said Pípa fiercely. 'If you do, I will tell Sanna straight away and we will catch you.'

'Then we will lose Oskar for ever!' hissed Mila.

Pípa's lip wobbled. 'I'm coming. I'll follow behind with Danya if you kick me off the sleigh. I'm coming.'

The moon was fully up. Mila looked at her sister's determined face in the moonlight, and could not think what to do. She could lock her in the dog shed, but Pípa would scream and set the dogs barking, and that would quickly bring the others running.

'Please,' she said to her sister. 'It's too dangerous for

you to come.'

Pípa stared at her, face implacable. 'I thought you were going to be late.' She pulled another bread roll from her cloak pocket and took a noisy bite.

Letting out a hiss of frustration, Mila harnessed Dusha to the sleigh. She thought a moment, then went back into the kennel to fetch Danya and harnessed him alongside his sister. With one more venomous glance at Pípa, she pushed off into the night. Things were already not going to plan, and she hadn't even left yet.

The meethouse was still bright and loud, and she steered them in a slow circle, keeping it out of sight. Pípa was silent as snow, and they reached the northern path. At the crossroads, Mila's heart sank. There was no light, no movement. But suddenly a crouched black rock shifted, and Rune's face looked up at them. He grimaced.

'What—?'

'My little sister,' said Mila apologetically.

Rune sighed heavily. 'This isn't a journey for such little ones.'

'I'm tall for my age,' said Pípa again, fiercely.

The two stared each other down for a moment, then Rune reached suddenly out for Pípa's hand. 'Is that yours?'

'My brother's,' said Pípa, holding up her hand for him to see the ring better. 'And my Papa's.'

'Shiny,' said Rune, looking thoughtful.

'You can't have it.'

'I don't want it.' He turned to Mila. 'At least you brought two dogs.' He slung his bundle on to the back of the sleigh and it clinked.

'I'm Pípa.'

'Rune. Is that bread?'

He settled beside Pípa, and Mila took this to mean the first driving shift was hers.

'Well,' said Rune, taking the roll Pípa held out to him. 'You know where to go.'

Mila took a deep breath and watched her exhalation smoke in the high moonlight. '*Farash!*'

The dogs gave a great leap forward and began to run.

Part 2
NORTH

Chapter Fourteen

Shadows

Frost glittered like finery on the bare branches of the trees: the night air was crystalline and bright. The stars were as thick as clouds above the branches, bunching over Mila's head.

She felt a bony hand on her shoulder, and out of the corner of her eye saw it was Rune, steadying himself.

'You're an excellent sleigh-driver.'

'The road is good,' Mila replied, the cold scratching her throat. Here the banks rose high on either side, and the snow had fallen and compacted between them, a thin skein of ice making the dogs scrabble.

'How far to Thule?' She felt ridiculous asking it, speaking the name of a story-island as though it were a real place. But they were going, and she had to believe there was something at the end of their journey.

'We must head for Bovnik first,' said the boy. 'It is our only path to the island.'

Mila's heart leapt at the mention of her mother's city. She glanced at Pípa's huddled form. Perhaps she could leave her little sister there – it would likely be safer than bringing her on the rest of the journey. 'All right, how far to Bovnik?'

Rune moved to stand at the rail beside her. He took one of the reins to balance the sleigh better.

'Three days' solid ride.'

Mila frowned, or at least she thought she did. Her forehead was numb. 'The dogs will need to rest.'

'I will help them,' said Rune. 'They will not need sleep.'

'Will it – doesn't it hurt them?'

'I thought we had decided to trust each other?'

Mila was not so sure about that. But she supposed something in her must trust him, or she would not be here, on this sleigh, riding to the top of the world, where the Bear waited. A thin keening came from the east, as if the wind were crying. A wolf.

She looked across at Rune. His moon eyes glittered. 'We will make it in time.'

'How can you be so sure?' said Mila impatiently.

Rune's thin face hardened.

'All you need to know – and trust – is that I want to help you, and that I can. I would not have given you hope if I could not get you there in time. But getting you there is all I can do – after that it's up to you.'

'What will I have to do?'

'You'll know.'

Mila highly doubted that, but in place of a reply an enormous yawn heaved itself out of her chest and stretched her mouth wide.

'Go and rest,' said Rune, slipping the other rein from Mila's grip. 'I will wake you at sunrise.'

Mila's eyes felt incredibly heavy all of a sudden. She made her careful way to the back of the sleigh, where Pípa lay piled beneath furs, her head on Rune's pack. Mila eased herself alongside her, and watched the forest whip past, trees as dark and high as walls.

Rune was whispering to the dogs, and the sleigh gave another wrench forward. Mila jammed her feet against the guard rail. They seemed to be going even faster, star streaks raking against the black-blue sky, but Mila was too weary to ask how Rune had managed it.

The trees were ghostly blurs. Mila turned her head to try and catch one in stillness, flicking her eyes back and forth, but it only made her dizzy, her eyelashes casting shadows at the corners of her vision. Then the shadows shifted, forming a vast dark shape moving between the trees, almost as fast as the sleigh.

Mila sat up as though hooked on a fishing line, a bitter taste filling her mouth. She stared at the trees again, searching for the shadowy shape. It was gone. Her heart thudded against her ribs. She had seen something, hadn't she? A wolf, perhaps . . . like the one she'd heard . . . but no. It had been too large, had moved with a lolloping stride.

A bear?

Pípa stirred in her sleep and Mila put a hand on her sister's warm side, feeling the soft rise and fall of her breath. Mila tried to slow her gasps to match as she stared out at the pale forest. She'd imagined it. She must have done. She lay back.

The night was the same colour as Sanna's hair, and Mila felt a stab of guilty satisfaction. It was Sanna who had always wanted to get away, and now she was the one left behind. She turned on to her side and curled against Pípa. Her little sister's hair had come loose from its plait and tickled Mila's nose. Mila closed her eyes and let the to and fro of the sleigh rock her to sleep.

She woke into early morning, the darkness lifting to let the sky lighten to grey. As her body stretched its way out of sleep, Mila realized that they were not moving. It must have been stopping that woke her. She lay looking at the

100

sideways trees creaking either side of a wide track, then lifted her head to turn them upright again.

'Rune?' The boy was standing hunched at the reins, and the dogs were whining their warning growl.

'Stay down.' Rune's tone was muted, as though he were trying to speak without moving his lips.

'What is it?' said Mila, instantly afraid, remembering the shadowy, lolloping shape. She peered past Rune, and saw a figure standing on the path before them.

It was tall, thin, cloaked, and unmoving as a tree.

The path was wide enough for two sleighs, but the figure stood in the very centre. They could not pass unless it moved.

Before she could take a closer look, Rune's boot kicked out and pushed Mila back down. She fell backwards into the furs, massaging her shoulder, but did not cry out.

'Can I help you, friend?' Rune's voice was as sharp and clear as frost.

No answer came. Rune hesitated a moment, then urged the dogs on at a walking pace. 'I need to pass this way. Would you mind stepping aside?'

Mila noticed Rune had said 'I'. He was trying to make the person believe he travelled alone, with only the dogs for company. She felt Pípa tug on her arm, and slid under the fur with her, holding her finger to her lips.

The last time she and Pípa had lain silent like this was when they had seen their brother at the ice window. Mila raised the furs a little, looked under the rail. She could see only the figure's legs. The bottom of the cloak was covered in ice, so thick she could make out the crystals bonded on top of one another, even at this distance. How long had the person been standing there? A small breeze flapped the long dark cloak about the figure's ankles, and Mila caught a flash of gold.

Chapter Fifteen

The Bound Boy

Her heart seemed to freeze. The figure was too small to be the Bear, but there was cord around its legs . . .

No. Mila looked more carefully as the cloak stirred in the wind. Only one leg was bound. As she saw this, Mila felt something hot pressing into her side. Trying to move as little as possible, she reached inside her cloak, and gave a small hiss of pain. The cord in her pocket was hot to the touch, like an ember not long pulled from a fire.

She took it out quickly, protecting her fingers with her cloak, and, even by the grey light filtering through a narrow gap in the furs, it was obvious the cord was once again shining and golden as heart tree sap. What had made it change? This person?

'What's that?' whispered Pípa, but Mila only clamped her hand over her sister's mouth.

'Please, move aside so I can pass,' came Rune's voice

again, but this time there was an undertow to his tone. Mila felt her own fear rising with Rune's. She pushed the golden cord back into her cloak, and reached for Oskar's knife at her belt.

They were three sleigh-lengths away from the figure before it finally spoke, in a deep, deliberate voice that sent icicles lancing into Mila's chest.

'I'd not go any further.'

It was the Bear's voice, she was sure of it. But this figure was not him – it seemed to be a boy not much older than Oskar. How did it have his voice? Mila strained to hear over her sister's rabbit-scared breaths.

'*Stuta*,' murmured Rune, bringing the dogs to a halt several paces away. 'I must, friend. My route is north.'

'Why are you travelling north in such cold? It's not safe for young ones.'

'I am not so young,' said Rune. Mila could tell he was trying to sound jovial, but his voice shook.

'Those two can't have seen many more winters between them than I have.'

'They're old enough in dog years,' tried Rune, as if he referred to Danya and Dusha, though the pretence was clearly useless. This boy knew Pípa and Mila were there. The gold cord seemed to grow hotter, its ember heat flaring. Mila kept her grip tight on Oskar's knife.

'Still,' said the boy in that terrible voice, 'one of them's old enough to be a thief.'

'We've nothing of yours,' said Rune. 'Let us pass in peace.'

'Only if Mila gives me back what's mine.'

Three things happened then, all at once.

Mila clasped a hand to her temple as she felt a stab of pain. Rune threw something – what, Mila had no idea; all she saw was the mage's hand arcing up. There was a smashing sound, and something black and glittering was falling about the boy's ankles. She smelt a chemical sharpness.

The figure began to cough and double over, Rune yelled, '*Farash!*' and Dusha and Danya began to run so fast and so suddenly it was as though a mighty current had them in its grip.

She and Pípa were thrown flat into the sleigh, and Mila kept her hand pressed to her head, eyes wide. It was similar to the pain she'd felt when Oskar had given her name to the Bear, like ice-head, the sort of pain she got from melting snow in her mouth.

The bound boy was not moving out of the way.

Worse than that, he was *trying* to move. He coughed and tugged at his unbound leg but, now they were nearly on top of him, Mila saw it was not only his cloak that was

105

icy – his legs were too.

He was frozen in place.

Rune seemed to notice at the same time. The mage tugged hard on the dogs' left rein, trying to steer around the figure, but the dogs swerved so sharply that they sent the sleigh skidding sideways towards him. Pípa screamed.

Mila closed her eyes as she felt rather than heard two sickening thuds as the iron-clad runners hit him, one after the other. The sleigh jerked up, and down, but did not break. Her body rose briefly into the air, and fell back hard, but she was numb to it.

All she could think of was binding Oskar's hand with lichen salve and balm leaves the month before, after he had cut himself sharpening the metal strips to make the sleigh grip better and run smoother. The runners were sharp as blades, and the sleigh was heavy with them and their supplies.

Rune swore and pulled the dogs to a stop. Pípa stopped screaming. Mila listened to the silence yawning beyond the caged drum of her heart. The cord in her pocket was cold again.

The boy had not even cried out.

After what felt like hours, but was only the length of one of Pípa's held breaths, the furs were lifted gently off Mila.

'Don't look,' said Rune, and his voice was as sad and tired as his crumpled face. 'I need my spare cloak.'

Mila could not think of anything worse than looking. She hated blood. Even binding Oskar's wound had turned her stomach, but she'd done it anyway. But, as in a night terror, she felt compelled to see the horror full in the face.

She pushed herself up, her back sore from the jolt of the collision, but Rune blocked her view with the cloak.

'No,' he said, more firmly. 'There are some things, Mila, that once you see them you cannot unsee, however much you wish it. You do not have to look.'

'We should bury him,' Mila replied, feeling shame at her relief. 'We killed him.'

'I killed him,' said Rune, and through her dull shock Mila saw that there were tears running down the mage's cheeks. 'And his face . . . he looked relieved. The Bear had him, and now he is at peace. You had nothing to do with it.'

'I did,' said Mila. She pulled the cord out of her pocket. 'He wanted this. Perhaps if I had given it to him—' Her throat tightened around her words.

'Hush,' said Rune, drawing Mila to him. He smelt of green spice and smoked apples. 'He was left here for one purpose only. To stop us.'

For that to happen, Mila thought, *the Bear must know we're following*. A splinter of fear lodged in her spine as she pressed her face into Rune's cloak and felt his bony collarbone. She could not bring herself to ask the mage to tell her whether she was right.

'He tried to move,' said Pípa. She was staring past them, and with horror Mila realized she was looking at the bound boy's body. 'He was trying to get away.'

Rune pulled Pípa to him as well, spreading his arms around them so the whole world was full of just the three of them, facing each other in the silent forest.

'This shows you what we are dealing with,' said Rune. 'The cord controls them, much like the names. Which reminds me –' Rune's voice became harsh – 'you lied to me.'

Mila blinked up at him, at those strange eyes, nearly light as snow. 'I—'

'You did not tell me he knew your name.'

Mila remembered the pain in her head, just before they struck the boy, triggered by her name in his mouth. She remembered too, hot shame warming her cheeks, how she had stayed silent when Rune said he could not help her if the Bear had her name.

'I didn't lie, exactly.'

'But you did not tell the truth,' said Rune gravely.

'You said you wouldn't help me!'

'And I wouldn't have.'

Queasiness planted its rocking foot in Mila's stomach. 'You . . . you aren't going to take us back?'

Rune looked at her for a long moment, then let out a longer breath. 'No. But there can be no more lies.'

'I'm sorry.'

Rune nodded, and squeezed her shoulder lightly. 'You two stay here. I'll be done in a minute. I'll move him off the road, cover him with snow. It's the best we can do.'

Pípa lay down in the sleigh. She was pale and trembling, and Mila again felt an awful guilt at allowing her to come. She took her sister's hand as she lay down beside her, and tried not to listen to the dogs whining, the sound of something heavy moving across the ice. Tried not to smell on the clean, fresh air the warm, metallic scent of blood, underlaid by the tang of whatever Rune had thrown at the figure. She clutched the cold cord and her sister's cold hand until Rune tapped her lightly on the shoulder. 'It's done.'

Mila looked instinctively at the mage's hands, but they were bare and washed with snow, no stain or mark on them. He held the gold cord from the boy's leg, which Mila knew would soon start to stiffen into something like a dead root.

'I thought it might be useful,' said Rune. 'I think you should keep it with the other.'

'Can't you—' started Mila, and immediately heard and hated the whine in her voice. 'All right.' She took the cord and hurriedly slipped it into her cloak.

She sat up, and saw Rune had swept fresh snow over the path. Only a shadow remained, sitting under the white like a slow-rising bruise.

Chapter Sixteen

The Chase

The sisters hugged each other close as Rune clucked his tongue, and Mila watched the patch of risen snow, set back from the road and topped with a cairn. Just before it disappeared out of sight, she thought the shadow stretching from under it moved. She shook her head, squeezing her eyes so tight stars danced inside her eyelids.

They rode silently for another hour or so, until Pípa's stomach gave such a mighty rumble Rune heard it from the front of the sleigh.

'*Stuta.*'

The mage rifled through his bags, and produced three parcels. He gave one to each of them, and Mila unwrapped it to find a crispbread and a whitish-yellow slab of a bitter-smelling cheese, which she assumed was made from Lunka's milk.

Rune sprinkled a little blackish-red herb on top of his

own crispbread, but on the sisters' he put something purple.

'What's that?'

'Moonroot, to help with the shock.'

'What's it do?' asked Pípa.

'It's soothing,' said Rune. 'I use it after a bad dream. You can also stuff a handful in your ears, and it blocks out all manner of sounds. It even stops me hearing Lunka snoring.'

'Who's Lunka?' giggled Pípa.

'His goat,' said Mila impatiently. 'Why do you have different?'

'Mine's got flameberry, for energy.'

Pípa bit and chewed. 'It's good, Mila! Like salt, almost.'

Mila could not think of anything she'd like to do less than eating, but Rune noticed her hesitation and looked at her sternly. 'You must be strong, Mila. You must eat.'

She bit into the cheese and crispbread. Pípa was right: it was beautifully salty. Rune nodded approvingly and bent to give the dogs some dried strips of meat, which he also scattered with flameberry.

'Is that—' Mila started, though Dusha was already wolfing hers down.

'It's safe,' said Rune reassuringly. He laid a careful

112

hand on her shoulder, his young face grave. 'We're on the same side, Mila.'

She nodded, cheeks flushing as she felt his pale eyes on her. She was starting to trust him. He made her feel safe, though he was scarcely more than a boy.

'Shall I take over the reins?' she asked, brushing crumbs from her cloak when they were finished.

'No,' said Rune. 'The flameberry will help me.'

Dusha was in a playful mood, snapping at Danya's heels and mock-growling. The flameberry had obviously helped them, too. Mila looked at Pípa, who was still pale. 'Sit with me, Mila?'

Mila slid back beside her little sister. Within moments of the dogs starting to run again, Pípa was asleep, her breath warming Mila's cheek. The trees whipped past overhead, making the light flicker, and when Mila closed her eyes she could almost imagine they were home again, with Oskar and Sanna, all lying together in front of the dancing fire.

There was heat on her cheeks – the sensation so forgotten and unfamiliar Mila did not immediately know it as different from cold. She placed her hand on her face and opened her eyes, but everything was so bright and searing she closed them instantly.

Something was wrong.

Mila blinked carefully. She could feel that they were moving, but she could not see that they were – no trees passing, branches whistling past. The world was bright, as though they were moving through the heart of a snow storm, but there was warmth on her face. The world was not white at all – it was burning.

Her forest was on fire!

Mila pushed herself up with a yelp, and saw then that she was mistaken. The forest was not on fire, because the forest was not there at all. She steadied herself against the side of the sleigh, willing herself to see the world as it was, things as they were.

There *were* trees, but they were sparse and scattered. Behind them, the thick line of the forest was far away, like a retreating tide. For the first time in Mila's life she could see for miles without a tree blocking her view.

A vast stretch of white sloped before her, dotted here and there with boulders and scraggy trees. Ahead was a peak, black as a fin and high as the heart tree. It was dizzying, sickening.

And there *was* fire, but it burned from the torches tied along the sides of the sleigh, and Mila now saw why they were lit. Amongst the scarce trees, black shapes darted, drawing closer and closer to the sleigh. A howl went up.

'Wolves!'

Mila hadn't meant to shout, but fear had gripped her throat and forced the word out. She tasted the metal of her fear as Rune turned.

'Oh, good, you're awake.' He sounded strangely calm. He still stood at the front rail of the sleigh, stiff as a statue. Beyond him, the dogs cut a deep path through the snow, dark bodies reassuringly solid against the white.

Mila felt winded, though all she had done was sit upright. The world had altered so entirely in the few hours she had slept. The forest was gone, the winter sun ghosting in the pale sky. Pípa was still sleeping.

'Wolves!' she repeated, pointing.

'I know,' said Rune. 'What do you think the torches are for?'

Mila stumbled to her feet. The world tipped again, the incline steep and unforgiving. Mila's legs went from under her as she lost her balance.

'What's wrong with you?'

'What's wrong with *me*?' Mila spat the horrid taste in her mouth over the side of the sleigh, ducking between the torches. 'What's wrong with *you*? Why didn't you wake us?'

'*Farash, farash!*' Rune whipped the reins. 'I can deal with the wolves. But seeing as you're up, you can help.'

'How long have I slept for?' asked Mila weakly.

'A bit over a day,' said Rune. 'You must have been tired.' He flicked a look over his shoulder. 'They're getting a bit too close for comfort.'

In her daze, Mila had almost forgotten the immediate danger, but as she followed Rune's gaze she saw that the immediate danger had not forgotten them. The wolves were no longer scattered amongst the far-off trees, but were running in a fast-closing semicircle, maybe a hundred feet behind.

Dusha and Danya were practically flying – Mila had never seen them run so fast, especially not sleigh-laden and uphill, but still they were no match for – *five, six, seven, eight!* – hungry wolves. The wind blew up behind them, and she could smell the tang of them, even over the torches – the burnt sweat-and-stale-blood excitement of the hunt. Mila looked more closely at them and her breath caught in her throat.

'Their eyes! They're—'

'Gold,' said Rune, almost to himself. His face went even paler. '*Javoyt!* They're his!'

'What do you mean?' Mila said wildly, though she already knew. She could feel the cords glowing again at her side.

'He's possessed them, like the boy. Take the reins!'

Mila stepped over Pípa, still deep in a moonroot sleep, and hurried to the front of the sleigh. Rune handed the leather reins to her and stood behind, speaking loudly in her ear.

'See the path? Off to the left?'

Her eyes scanned the mountains to the north-east. They looked as steep and impossible as a wave. She shook her head.

'There!' Rune pointed and Mila looked along his arm, and suddenly she did see: a thin imprint sunk between two crests, like the gap between Pípa's front teeth.

'Yes!'

Rune moved to the back of the sleigh. Mila blinked and the path disappeared as if it had never been, but with the next blink it was back, a mere speck in the distance. Mila adjusted the reins, pulling the dogs slightly left. '*Farash*, Dush-Dush! *Farash*, Danya!'

Dusha gave two great barks at the sound of her voice, and the dogs' ears went back. They sped as fast and straight as spears, the points of their noses arrowing forward. Mila chanced a look around, and immediately wished she hadn't.

The wolves were barely twenty paces behind, and as the incline became steeper, they seemed to speed up, leaping chaotically over one another, gold eyes flashing.

Rune was crouched by Pípa's head, and Mila could see her sister was now awake and gripping tightly on to the sleigh.

'Come on, come on.' The mage was muttering and pulling object after object out of his bundle, vials and flints and boxes and scarves, until, 'Aha!'

He held up his hand. Something black glinted in his grasp and Mila guessed it was the same powder he'd thrown at the boy. She pulled her gaze back to the path, correcting Dusha and Danya's direction. They were getting close to the pass, and Mila could see that a great slab of snow overhung it, creating a tunnel for them to pass through and down the other side of the mountain.

'Could you get them to go a little faster?' called Rune.

Mila ground her teeth. A snarl came curling into her ear and she looked to her right. A lone wolf galloped alongside, grey and black, yellow teeth bared. Mila had a soft spot for wolves. Though they rarely sighted them in Eldbjørn forest, they looked so like her beloved dogs, only thinner and fiercer. But these were the Bear's.

She steered the dogs quickly right and then left, sending the sleigh whipping sideways. She felt a small *bump* and her stomach soured, remembering two sickening thuds, the bloody shadow under the snow. The wolf yelped and fell away. When Mila looked back over her shoulder she saw it stop completely, but it was still standing, still alive.

'Well done,' cried Rune. 'But hold straight and fast as we go over!'

The pass was as close in front as the wolves were behind.

'Ready?' called Rune, and Mila nodded, though she did not know if the mage was looking or what she was ready for. A moment later she saw the black vial go sailing over her head and lodge in the powdery snow of the overhang. As they passed beneath it Mila shouted again, '*Farash!*' and the dogs pelted on.

The ground dropped away beneath them and Mila felt the weightlessness of flight as the sleigh's momentum sailed them downwards. She held tight to the handle of the sleigh, turning her head in time to see Rune thrust a burning torch into the overhanging snow.

There was a burst of bright white light, and a bang so loud Mila felt it in her bones. She heard Pípa scream and she forced her eyes open, looking around for her sister. The ground rushed up to meet them.

Chapter Seventeen

Buried

S now in her nose and mouth, snow in her ears and eyes. She was drowning in it. Mila spat and worked her hand free from where it was clamped to her side, bringing it up to clear a hollow beside her mouth so she could breathe. She scraped snow from between her lips and gums, and snorted to clear her nose. All around her was dark grey, the colour of light gulleted through thick snow.

Her heart was pounding, and the blood rushed to her head. Something was pressing around her neck, and she realized her cap had slipped backwards, the leather tie tightening around her throat. *Breathe*, she thought, but it was just as irritating as someone else saying it.

Remember what to do. Her father's voice floated to her on a tide of panic. *If you're buried in a snow crush, the first thing to do is find out which way is up.*

Mila was sure that this was what had just happened.

That mad mage had started a snow crush. Whatever had been in that black vial had reacted with the fire, and buried them all. *Pípa.*

She forced herself to think clearly. *Which way is up?*

Mila cleared a bigger hollow by her mouth, and spat again, this time paying attention to where the spit fell. It dripped sideways, towards her left cheek, which meant that that was downwards. She flexed her trapped legs, and they responded. Her ribs ached but her limbs seemed unbroken. Her thick layers of furs must have helped.

Make space for yourself, gently, so the snow doesn't pack tighter. Move your arms and legs as if you're making a snow bird.

She began to gently work her limbs back and forth, freeing them. Her breath was coming faster and faster, but she forced it into a steady rhythm. Being buried in snow was like being trapped in earth and drowning in water – she had air, but it was limited. She had movement, but it was limited.

Move slowly, and keep your breathing calm.

Once her legs were loose enough, she drew them up to her torso, wiggling her toes to get the blood moving. At least she still had both her boots – if she made it out of here, she would need her feet, and in snow a lost boot meant a lost foot.

I need to get to Oskar. A gasp gripped her throat, a burst of missing so sharp it seemed to pierce her skin. She forced it down and began to wriggle away from the direction her spit had fallen. Upwards.

Using her hands like shovels, she swept the snow sideways so it dropped downwards. There, she kicked it into compact ridges and used her feet to push off them, until she was climbing the hollow left by her body.

It felt achingly slow, but Mila counted to one hundred, and counted to one hundred again, and at two hundred and forty-three her hand was gripped by biting cold, and then a warm wetness against her exposed wrist.

As she pulled herself clear, a great panting weight collapsed on her, and she realized Dusha was on top of her, covering every part of her face with licks.

'It's all right, Dush-Dush. Good girl.'

Her harness was still attached, but all Mila could see of the sleigh was a snapped-off wooden ring. She eased the dog off her, held on to her harness and Dusha pulled her to her feet.

Mila swayed and blinked the world into focus. The snow crush had reduced the smooth side of the mountain to a choppy mess, and all about her were more peaks. It was still light and she was certain she hadn't lost consciousness, which meant she'd not been buried long.

She looked up behind them. There was no sign of the wolves, but snow was still scattering from the shattered overhang, blocking the path through.

'Mila!'

Her heart filled suddenly at the sound of Pípa's voice, and she turned to see the small dark dot of her sister further down the slope, Danya sitting loyally by her side. Mila felt choked by relief, and threw herself downwards, Dusha bounding alongside. She flung herself beside Pípa, holding her tight.

'Are you hurt?' she said, gripping her sister's shoulders and looking into her eyes for signs of the wide pupils that meant concussion.

Pípa shook her head. 'Only a bit buried.' She pointed to her leg, which was cut off at the knee by snow.

Mila began to dig her out, and Dusha joined in, sending snow flying, while Pípa chattered on. 'I woke up and I was flying, Mila! And the mountain was falling, and I held on to Danya's harness, and he ran me clear. You weren't there, but I called and called and now you are.'

'You should know better than to call after a snow crush,' Mila scolded half-heartedly as she pulled her sister's leg free, and Pípa lay back as though making a snow bird. 'You might've have set it off again. Where's Rune? Have you seen him?'

Pípa shook her head, suddenly tearful. 'I couldn't see any of you. But the sleigh's over there.' She pointed further up the slope. 'That's where Dusha came from. She was digging there when you came out.' She threw herself forward and hugged Mila painfully. 'I'm really glad you're here, Mila.'

Mila kissed the top of her head. 'Me too. Let's go, Píp. I have to check the sleigh.' She looked around and saw they were in a ravine, with a crown of mountains rising up on all sides. They were lucky Rune hadn't brought the whole range down on their heads. Beyond them, yet more mountains stretched north in a long range.

'You go with Danya, up the side there, in case any more snow comes loose.'

She helped Pípa to her feet, patted Danya and waited for them to reach the ridge before she trudged back up towards the lump of the sleigh, pulling her fur cap back on to her head. It was slightly damp, but better than the funnelled chill wind that started to gnaw at her ears.

Dusha trotted alongside, trailing her broken harness. The snow was loose and dangerous beneath their feet, and Dusha was careful to stay beside Mila, so she could hold on to her when she sank too deep.

Finally, they reached the sleigh. It looked like a shipwreck – all their bundles scattered, clothes strewn like seaweed, planks of wood sprouting here and there. One of the rails stuck out of the snow at a right angle, like a mast.

It had flipped over completely, and Mila rubbed the soft spot at the base of Dusha's ears, glad that she had broken free. To be caught up in the wreck of the sleigh would probably have meant being crushed.

Rune.

Dusha nuzzled her side, and then went to dig beside the sleigh again. Mila swallowed hard, kneeling to join her. The dog had already made good progress in the soft snow, and before long Mila felt the guard rail where the torches had been tied.

She felt along its length, left and right, scooping out the loose powder until the whole length of the sleigh was uncovered. She stuck her hand through the gap of the guard rail and—

Something grabbed back.

'Mila?'

'Rune,' said Mila, heart racing. 'Give me my hand back!'

She felt relief and annoyance and anger all mushed up and boiling inside her. When Rune released her grip she smacked her hand on top of the upturned sleigh.

'Ow, that's loud!'

Mila banged it again. 'Why did you start the snow crush? Pípa could have been killed!'

'She's all right?'

'Yes, but she might have been hurt! We all could have been.'

'And yet here you are, making a racket fit to deafen even those in the halls of the dead.'

'Of all the stupid, unthinking—'

Rune's hand shot out of the gap and grabbed Mila's wrist again. 'The wolves, Mila. I had to stop the wolves.'

'But you didn't need to bring the mountain down.'

Rune chuckled. 'These mountains have withstood worse than a little brimstone.'

'That's what that was?' said Mila, relaxing her wrist into Rune's grasp. 'It smelt so . . . bright.'

'Sparks pretty bright too,' said Rune. 'It bought us time. I'm sorry for scaring you, Mila, truly. And I am glad you and Pípa are all right.'

Mila could feel her eyes brimming and she wiped them hurriedly, glad the mage could not see. 'I'm glad you're all right, too.'

'Mila?' Pípa's voice came thin and echoing over to them. 'Why are you talking to the sleigh?'

Mila felt a laugh bubble up. 'It's Rune, he's underneath.'

'And he'd like to get out now,' came the mage's

muffled voice.

Mila led Dusha to the other side of the sleigh and tied her trailing harness to the guard rail.

'When I say, curl up,' said Mila. 'We're going to flip the sleigh.' She placed her hands underneath the rail and looked at Dusha, who stared back, tongue lolling, waiting for instruction. 'Now! *Farash!*'

Dusha cantered away, Mila heaved upwards, and the sleigh came off Rune in a great rush. The boy lay swirled like a sleeping dog.

'*Stuta!*' called Mila, and Dusha came to a stop as Mila helped Rune to his feet, letting go as soon as the boy was steady. Her relief that they were all unhurt was fading fast now she saw what a state the sleigh was in. The sealskin bed was split in two, and one of the rails sat at a right angle to the sleigh. Heat flooded her numb cheeks. 'Now what?'

Rune blinked at her.

'Now what?' she hissed again.

'We keep going.' The mage frowned. 'What else would we do?'

'The sleigh is ruined!' Mila said accusingly. 'I don't know why you had to come! It would have been faster on my own. On my own, my dogs could've outrun the wolves—'

'Oh, no, they couldn't,' interrupted Rune.

'The sleigh's ruined,' repeated Mila bitterly.

'We don't need the sleigh.' Rune started gathering their scattered belongings.

Mila looked down the slope, at Pípa throwing snowballs for Dusha and Danya to chase. The dogs were running full pelt after them, returning confused and empty-mouthed. It was a strangely peaceful scene, so different from minutes before. Mila shuddered, remembered the wolves' yellow teeth, their golden eyes, so like the Bear's. A sudden thought occurred to her.

'Rune?'

'Mmm?' He was packing another of his bags.

'How did the Bear know to leave the boy? To send the wolves? Does he . . . ?' A lump rose in her throat. 'Does he know we're following?'

Rune looked up slowly. 'I have been thinking the same. We can only hope he left them to make the route difficult for anyone taking it, rather than us specifically.' Mila did not feel reassured. Rune reached out and squeezed her arm. 'Don't worry. It's likely he doesn't know.'

'Why?'

'Because he'd come and finish the job himself.'

Mila gulped.

'Are we going or not?' Pípa called, stamping her feet. Mila jumped and looked around, raising her finger to her lips to shush her sister. 'I warned her not to shout after a snow crush!'

She turned back to Rune, but the mage was hastily gathering the last of his things.

'Rune, what if you—?'

'Pípa's right, we should get going.'

Mila wanted to ask more, but there was a finality in Rune's tone that told her it would be hopeless. Besides, there was no time. They had to get to Oskar.

She gathered what was most necessary: food, anything warm, and helped Rune wrench the broken rails from the sleigh.

Pípa trudged to meet them with the dogs, and Rune unearthed his parcel of food and gave them each a slice of black bread with flat, round seeds that Mila had never had before. On top he sprinkled flakes of flameberry. It tasted a bit like moss, but in a good way.

After the meal, they wrapped their possessions in the ripped sealskin and Rune tied it on to his back. Mila and Rune lifted the rails parallel to each other, stopping them from sliding away with bundled clothes.

The mage knelt and tied Pípa's boots to the detached rails first. Next he tied Mila's, and finally his own. They'd placed the dogs one in front of another, and now Rune gave Mila the reins. Mila wrapped her arms either side of Pípa and took a deep breath. *There must be no more delays*, she thought. *We must get to Oskar.*

'Ready?' said Rune.

'Ready!' cried Pípa, sounding so brave and definite Mila felt a lump of pride rise in her throat. She squeezed her gently, then scanned the mountains ahead. She fixed the path in her sights and gripped the reins, the snapped leather squeaking against her gloves. She filled her lungs with freezing air. 'Ready!'

Chapter Eighteen

The Pass

Cold hovered like a carrion bird. The higher they went, the thinner the air, and it seemed to Mila the cold took on the shadowy presence of a crow, circling over her, finding her exposed wrists, the soft parts beneath her ears and at the base of her neck. It perched on her shoulders, making them heavy and stiff, dug needles of pain into her joints, buried its beak at her pulse points, cawing ice through her veins.

Mila saw now what a luxury a sleigh was, absorbing most of the unevenness of the ground. Now she felt each jolt of the rocky terrain. The wind moaned through her cap, crept up her nostrils and gummed into her eyes, making them stream hot tears that froze into gritty ice dust. The knots Rune had tied around her ankles bit tight, and her legs felt sore and cramped from the slight bend needed to stop the jolts shaking her knees out of place.

'Are you all right?' she asked, leaning forward to whisper the question to Pípa. Her little face was so bundled in furs all Mila could see were her bright brown eyes, streaming like hers. She nodded, and Mila twisted her head to speak out of the corner of her mouth to Rune.

'Will we ski through the night?'

'No choice,' said the mage. He was being short with her, Mila could feel it, ever since she had asked about the Bear following them. What was he hiding? What was he so afraid to tell her?

Mila drew the dogs back to a fast trot over the icy steps of the mountainside. The wind dropped a little here, nestled against the shoulder of the mountain, and Mila again looked up and up at its jagged teeth, wondering what it must be like to stand at the top and see all of the world stretched out beneath you.

'Have you been here before?' she called over her shoulder to Rune.

'Yes.'

Mila sighed and turned forward again, but the mage seemed to relent and continued, 'I love the mountains. I love being up high.'

'I'm not so sure about it.'

'Nor me,' said Pípa.

'I think I was a gyrfalcon once. Or perhaps I will be

some day, in another life.'

'You think you will be a bird in another life?' scoffed Mila.

'My mother and grandmother became bird spirits,' said Rune smoothly. 'I suspect I will be no different.'

'You really believe your family turned into birds when they died?'

'You're taking us too far to the west. The smoother course is further right.'

Mila corrected the dogs and waited for Rune to reply, but he had fallen silent again. Mila let the silence stretch, focusing on the ascent. Finally, the dogs reached the summit and she pulled on the reins. '*Stuta.*'

She saw now that it was the way of mountains to carry on outdoing each other. Like in a forest, where the tallest trees vied for the sky – here the mountains seemed to graze the sky itself. The mountain they had climbed now seemed more of a hill – and what faced them was a ridge, barely wider than their skis. Mila thought she could see impressions in the snow, and thought of Oskar fighting through the biting wind. She flicked a look behind them, twisting as far as she could with her legs bound in place. At least the snow crush had stopped the wolves following.

'Is that . . . north?' said Pípa, hesitantly.

The air felt even thinner here and Mila was struggling to breathe, though all she'd done was hold steady while the dogs laboured. She shivered, and Rune squeezed her shoulder.

'Let's not delay. If we're lucky we can traverse it before sunset.'

As soon as Mila started the dogs again, a wind hit them from the east, funnelling through a gap in the peaks and smelling of wet stone and cold copper. It was a blunt wind, coming in one great slamming gust. They made themselves as small as possible as the dogs drew them forward.

She felt Dusha and Danya's uncertainty – their shoulders rolled lower to the ground, as if they wanted to slide along on their bellies. But Dusha was the braver, and soon her brother was matching her stride, drawing closer and closer to the cloud line.

Towards late afternoon a shadow split the snow before them, and Pípa gasped.

'Look up, Mila, look up!'

Mila tilted back her stiff neck. Above them swirled a shadowy shape. It seemed black against the grey clouds but then it dipped and Mila saw two great wings, their span wider than her outstretched arms even at this distance, and then the twist of a feathered head.

An eagle, larger than any she'd seen before, circling. Mila's stomach swooped as the bird did. And then, the cords began to warm. Mila felt them through her cloak, like a brand. The eagle's shadow crossed them – a great, dark cloud – and grew bigger and bigger against the snow. Mila looked up just in time to see the eagle swooping closer. Its head tilted, and its eye glinted an unnatural gold.

'*Javoyt!*' A muttered curse came from behind her, and Rune reached forward to seize the reins from her. 'Heads down!' the mage cried. '*Farash!*'

The dogs shot forward so fast Mila had to almost bend double over Pípa.

'It's him again, isn't it?' cried Pípa wildly. Mila's answer was muffled by her sister's hat, and she pulled her close. Through streaming eyes she saw they were approaching the clouds, the incline leading them into the sky. Rune was taking them blind into it – there was no telling if the ridge carried on straight or veered off left or right.

The shadow, faint in the low light, circled again and again, growing all the time. Then, sudden as a gust of wind, it grew enormous, and Mila felt a rush against her face, heard a crack of wings beating, and Rune cried out in pain.

'Get away!'

A blow caught the back of Mila's head, hard as a punch, and she reeled, seeing through bright spots of pain that the reins were loose and flapping, that the dogs were slowing and straying towards the ridge edge.

The eagle had attacked them! She grasped for the reins, but they whipped about her feet, and she could not reach them. She blinked hard, trying to steady her vision as Rune gasped and swore behind her.

Just as suddenly, the dogs were speeding up and running straight again.

'Faster, Danya! *Farash*, Dusha!'

Pípa had seized the reins and was urging them on, her high voice ringing out like a bell across the mountains, Papa's ring glinting on her thumb as she whipped the reins again and again. Mila wanted to reach for Oskar's knife but dared not let go of Pípa. If she shifted her weight too far, all of them would plunge off the ridge.

Again the eagle's shadow loomed to one side, and Mila saw a blackish glint fly past her towards it. Rune had thrown one of his brimstone vials. The eagle screeched as the black glitter burst in its gold eyes, and wheeled away.

'*Farash!*' screamed Pípa, and the dogs responded yet again. Up they rose and up.

Mila gasped as they broke the chill mist of the cloud bank. It was like hitting a foaming current. The cold

seeped deep inside her, the way ice splits the cracks in rock and breaks them outwards. It seemed to lick around her very bones.

She looked desperately about her, but in the mist she could barely see beyond her own nose. After a while she gently tapped her sister's shoulder.

'*Stuta*,' whispered Pípa, and the dogs came to a panting stop. All three of them crouched down. Mila's thighs began to quake, and Rune placed gentle hands beneath her armpits to take her weight. All Mila could see was white, all she could hear was the black howl of the wind that brought the cloud swirling about them.

They stayed crouched down until Mila could have thought her body stone if it weren't for the pain radiating from the eagle's blow. Pípa was holding her breath, and Mila tightened her arms around her, burying her face in Pípa's scarf until she could feel her sister's pulse, beating as fast as a snared rabbit's.

Finally, Rune released his grip on Mila, pushing her gently up. In turn, Mila pushed Pípa, and they stood upright, calves cramping in their bindings.

'I th-think it's g-g-gone,' said Pípa, a chatter in her teeth knocking the words loose.

'We have to move.' Mila tried to uncurl her sister's fingers from the reins. 'Let go, Pípa. It's all right.'

Pípa began to shake, and Mila longed to untie her feet and pick her up, hold her like a baby. She should never have brought her, never have allowed her to come on such a dangerous and uncertain journey.

A fierce, bubbling self-loathing swelled inside her, and she swallowed it down. There was no time. Somewhere, beyond the edge of possibility, their brother was bound in gold, trapped by a vengeful spirit. They had to reach him. This could not all be for nothing.

She heard Sanna's sharp laugh in her head. *Yes, hurry up, Mila. Before the Bear steals our brother's soul. Because that is perfectly possible, isn't it?*

Mila straightened, her spine clicking painfully, resolve tightening like a noose. *I'll save him, Sanna. You wait and see.*

Chapter Nineteen

Bovnik

The sun had been sinking fast before they entered the cloud, and all around them it was growing darker. Mila took the reins and started the dogs again. Their tails lifted and they strained forwards, the reins taut as fishing lines, making Mila glad of her thick gloves.

Finally, they broke the cloud cover. She looked all about them for the eagle, but there was no sign of it. The skies were empty above them: no birds, no clouds, nothing. What there was instead was a changed world. Pípa gave a whistle through her teeth.

'This . . . this . . .'

She stopped, because there were no words for this. The sun was sinking to the west, staining the sky orange as cloudberries. Before them was a sea of clouds, peaks of mountains marooned here and there beneath the endless, endless sky that was nothing like the sky Mila knew, its twilight grey lightening at noon before folding them into dark again. This was a sunset full of colour, though not warmth. And she had never seen, she realized now, the horizon.

But there it was. The edge of the world meeting some other edge, and the sun, sinking into it. And was that a break in the ice? An island, shimmering like frost on the northern horizon, hovering between this world and the next? Mila squinted, but the ice was bright and made her eyes smart.

'Is that Bovnik?' Pípa was pointing to the near distance. 'Where Mama was from?'

Draped across twin peaks ahead, like the roots of a jewelled tree, were the sparse lights of the near-abandoned city. Roofs glimmered in the sunset, and Mila remembered how Mama had told them it seemed the mountains pierced the sun at sunset and sent its light dripping down the buildings. And spun above it all was the trading platform, balanced like a playing card between the mountains.

'This is where the colour hides,' said Rune. His voice sounded weak and faraway. Mila remembered the blow of the eagle, and wondered if it had caught Rune, too.

Bovnik grew brighter as the sun dropped. The city was built facing north-west, to enjoy the long evenings of summers that had long since ceased to arrive. She could imagine the sun striking the city as Mama had said, colouring it gold and orange.

The road was cut into the mountainside, wide enough for two eight-dog sleighs to pass each other, and ski runnels were worn deep into glossed ice, making the going quick and smooth. As they came to a wide curve, the sun flooded the horizon and was gone all at once.

'Should we stop?' asked Mila. She didn't like the idea of continuing in the dark, however good the road.

'It's strange,' said Rune. 'It should have been lit by now. Wait.' She heard him rummaging for something. He pulled out a vial of brimstone and threw it at a trough set into the mountainside. The trough caught fire in both directions.

'How—?'

'Oil,' said Rune, as Mila gasped and watched the fire spread around the mountain and out of sight. 'Used to be that the torchbearer lit it at sundown every night.' He sounded worried.

'Oil? They burnt it just for light?'

'They had plenty of everything,' said Rune. 'They thought such waste a good thing – an impressive thing.'

Mila could tell by Rune's tone that he was not impressed, but she was. It was a waste – of course it was – but it was also clever, and comforting, to have light to navigate the road by.

'Have you been here before?'

'My spirit has.'

Pípa gave a little snort. 'Your spirit?'

'Mm. You know when you have dreams that you are flying?'

'Yes.'

'It's like that, except my spirit is actually flying.'

'Or you're just dreaming,' muttered Pípa, so quietly only Mila could hear.

They curled around the mountain, below the houses they had sighted from the ridge. Only a handful had lights burning from their small round windows. They were shaped like beehives, curving out from the mountainside.

'They're caves,' explained Rune. 'They're built out from the natural breaks in the rock. The curved walls stop the wind taking hold and ripping them out.'

Mila imagined huge hands raking the mountainside, reaching inside the hive-homes like a bear seeking honey. A chill slithered down the length of her body as she remembered the eagle plunging at them, and a deep voice speaking her name, a hand reaching into her head and squeezing like a vice.

Finally they reached a set of gates, carved into the rock

and lit by two huge torches. Mila pulled the dogs to a stop. Rune untied his feet and stepped from the skis. He walked to a grating in the rock that Mila would not have noticed, and reached through. Mila heard the sound of a lever being pulled, and then there was a creaking, grinding noise, as loud as thunder, and the gates began to open in the middle.

'You'd think they could spare some oil to grease the hinges,' whispered Mila, and Pípa giggled, but Rune's face was grave as he knelt to untie Pípa's ankles.

'We'll walk from here. You two stay quiet and stay close.'

Mila released the dogs from their harnesses and they shook themselves, melted ice whipping off their fur. Dusha yawned, then came to stand beside her, while Danya went to Pípa.

'Good girl, Dush-Dush,' murmured Mila, placing her hand on her warm, soft head as they stepped into the city. Her legs were weak after all the skiing, and walking felt as strange as swimming. It was odd how quickly her body had adjusted to the crouch of skiing, to the thinner air.

'Where is everyone?' said Rune, almost to himself. The mountain was ridged and tiered. The tier they stood on was the widest, jutting out from the mountain on a ledge of rock. The houses looked even more like hives up close, their rounded walls as smooth as paper. The next, narrower tier overhung them by some fifty feet, and Mila saw it was made of wood, struts criss-crossing above them. But there was no one in sight.

'Perhaps they left when winter came,' said Mila. Mama had told them how treacherous the mines were in winter.

'Or perhaps the Bear scared them away,' said Pípa. 'Did your spirit dreams not show you it was abandoned?'

'They did not,' said Rune, seemingly missing the tease in her voice. 'At least it makes going up easier, no one to ask questions.'

Easier for the Bear, too, Mila thought, as she craned her neck. 'How do you get up?'

'There are steps,' said Rune.

He started walking but Mila hung back. She wasn't here for a tour.

'How do we get to Thule?'

'You'll see,' said Rune quietly. 'Let's go.'

Chapter Twenty

The Climb

As they made their way to the steps, a few faces peered at them through the windows. They were thin and furtive-eyed, looking away as soon as Mila turned her gaze on them. They were too busy surviving here, Mila supposed: no one was interested in them, nor even in a man the height and width of a bear.

The city brought a wave of homesickness crashing over her. She missed the forest; even after Papa had left, there had always been the four of them. Four people who promised to care for each other no matter what. She could not imagine living in a place where you didn't care who or what was around you.

We must rescue Oskar, she thought, fiercely. *Things must be as they were.*

They passed the open door of some stables, and when Mila peered inside she saw a dozen ponies drinking from a trough and eating from piles of frozen hay. One stood larger than all the rest, a horse with a black mane and tail.

'I think these are his!' Mila exclaimed. 'The boys were on ponies. And he was on that one.'

Rune doubled back to look in. 'Probably. He takes what he needs, and leaves it when he no longer requires it. They'll be taken care of, though. There are still some people here, did you see? Probably too poor to leave.' He looked around. 'We should leave the dogs here, too.' Dusha was already sniffing and straining towards the trough. 'They can look after the bags while we climb.'

Mila's hand tightened on Dusha's harness. She'd not thought about this, though of course they couldn't come to Thule.

'They will be safe here,' said Rune gently.

Mila nodded and sank to her knees, wrapping her arms around Dusha's neck and breathing in her warm biscuity smell. 'Be good, Dush-Dush.'

Dusha whined in the back of her throat and nuzzled in deeper to Mila's embrace. Pípa hugged Danya, and then the sisters led their dogs to the trough. Rune began shedding bags, taking out vials and several strange orbs, placing them in a pouch attached to his belt until he clinked like a rusted hinge.

'What're those?' asked Mila, pointing to the orbs. They looked a bit like soap bubbles, only with thicker outsides.

'Breath-skeins,' said Rune, leaving Mila none the wiser. She checked she had Oskar's knife and the two pieces of golden cord before leaving her bag in the corner of the stable too.

Dusha and Danya were still drinking, and Rune pulled on her arm.

'Come now,' he said softly. 'While they're distracted. It's easier.'

She nodded mutely and let herself be led away by Pípa while Rune shut the door. There was a tearing inside her chest. While Dusha and Danya were with them, it was like travelling with a piece of home. She tightened her grip on Pípa's hand.

They reached the steps, which were more like a ladder, a slice of lighter grey rock cut at foot-high intervals into the mountainside. The steps dipped slightly in the middle from years of use, and looked perilously slippery, though the torches burning at intervals were keeping them free of ice.

'Why do the platforms not catch fire?' asked Pípa.

Rune frowned at her. 'What do you mean?'

Pípa pointed. 'They're wooden. Isn't it dangerous to

have the torches so close?'

'They're not wood. They're bone.'

'No one has bones that big.'

'Whales do,' said Rune. 'The largest ones are their ribs.'

Mila's eyes widened. She could see now that the struts of the platform were curved, and overlaid crossways with smaller bones. *Whales.* Mama had told her they were huge, that one catch could feed and keep the torches of whole villages lit for weeks, but still Mila had never imagined something that had bones the size of trees inside them.

She pictured something that large floating – *how massive the sea must be to have hundreds of whales in it!* – opening a mouth as wide as a ship, its tongue the size of a sail. It would render even Sanna speechless. She placed her hands either side of her own chest. Even in her thick cloak and winter vest, her whole ribcage did not match the width of one of those bones.

'Let's climb,' Rune said.

Mila's legs were sore from skiing, and she was overcome by the scale of the whalebones. She simply did not see how it would be done – the climb, the rescue – any of it.

She tried to put it from her mind, tried to focus on the movement of arm, then leg, then other arm, other leg, the pull and push of the slow ascent, her ragged breathing. *Don't look down.* Anyway, Rune had brought them this far. If it weren't for him, Mila would still be in Stavgar, sure that Oskar had not left her willingly but uncertain how to follow him.

Finally they reached the trading platform. Mila's arms shook. No matter how deep she breathed, she could not take in enough air. Pípa looked in similar pain, clutching her ribs. The air was tangibly thinner, full of the salt of the sea, leaving her lungs gasping for more. Rune pulled himself gracefully over the top and stood, breathing steadily. He did not seem tired at all.

'We made it,' he said, and Mila looked about them. The trading platform was empty, just a vast expanse over the empty maw of the mine. A strange creaking sound, a bit like the gates opening, wafted up to them: the sea, groaning in its cage of ice. There were no torches here, but they did not need them, because the sky was shot through with stars, more stars than she had ever seen.

Here and there were what looked like clouds, but were stardust, fine as gossamer, stretched over the dazzle and shine. The sky was actually glowing, not in the way it sometimes did with the sky fire, the coloured flames that licked the sky on especially cold and clear nights, but as if the sun had been shattered and scattered into a thousand fragments.

At home Mila's view of the heavens was obscured by trees – slices of sky with trees overlaid like fingers over her eyes – but here it felt as if she were in a giant upended bowl, perforated with light. From horizon to horizon, she could see stars, and there, to what must be the north, something glassy shimmered. The frozen Boreal Sea. And was that something solid, a smudge of land on the far-off horizon?

'Is that . . . ?'

Rune narrowed his pale eyes, more moon-like than ever in the crisp winter starlight. He seemed to freeze, only his breath betraying movement.

'Is that Thule?'

He nodded.

'How do we get to it?'

Rune pointed to a wide crevasse to their right, fenced off by a rope. Mila went and peered down.

And down.

And down.

She gripped the rope, her balance faltering as though she stood on a ship at sea, not solid rock. A waterfall was skimming down the mountain, and far, far below them a river was flowing beneath ice, white foam crashing against rocks, the water racing faster than Mila could run.

'A river?'

Mila traced the course of the river until it sliced out of sight into the night. North. To the Boreal Sea, choked with ice. And caught in its grip was an island, where her brother waited.

'Don't we need a boat?' She stepped back, unsteadily. 'Do we have to break the ice? Why did we climb up?'

'We have to find the right current. The current the Bear placed there to reach Thule.'

'The right current? How will we know it?'

Rune smiled. 'It's the Bear's favourite colour. But you can only reach it if you have enough speed.'

She eyed the waterfall, his words sinking in. 'We have to jump?' The mage was untying his belt, head bowed. 'Rune?'

He took out five of the orbs – the breath-skeins – from his pouch and attached them to the belt, then held it out. '*You* have to jump.'

Mila stared, uncomprehending. 'You're . . . you're not coming?'

He wasn't looking at her.

'Rune, why aren't you coming?'

'Because there's something I have to do here,' he said, finally raising his head to meet her eyes. His gaze was steady, full of sorrow. 'I can't explain, but you have to go on alone.'

'She won't be alone,' said Pípa, taking Mila's hand, but Mila shrugged her off, still staring at the mage.

'What do you have to do?'

Rune stepped forward and looped the belt around her waist. She stared dumbly down at his hands as they buckled it, listened to his gentle words: 'Trust me, Mila. And listen – these are all the things you will need. When you enter the waterfall, use the breath-skeins. Then, when you reach Thule . . .'

Mila heard Rune through the rising buzz of blood in her ears. She did not want to do this without him. She could not do this without him. As he described what they would find in Thule – strange and terrible things – she wanted to scream, to shout at him and shake him until he agreed to not make them face them alone.

'Do you understand, Mila?' He was standing very close to her, still smelling of apple smoke and herbs. He took her hands gently. 'Repeat it back to me.'

But at that moment she felt a warmth begin to pulse at her side and she gasped, pulling away from the mage. She placed her hand in the pocket of her cloak and felt that the cords were warm, just as they had been when the frozen figure was near, the wolves and the eagle. They were pliable too, and she drew one out. It glowed.

Rune and Mila locked eyes, fear reflected in them as Pípa stepped towards the stone steps, eyes wide with shock.

'Sanna!'

Chapter Twenty-One

The Drop

Mila wheeled around, certain Pípa must be mistaken, or seeing things. But there, hauling herself over the final stone step, dressed in her blue dress and fur-trimmed cloak clasped by Geir's brooch, was their eldest sister. She stood up and looked straight at Mila. Her face was thunderclouds and lashing rain.

'Sanna!' called Pípa again.

Mila took a step back even as Pípa rushed forward to clutch Sanna's skirts. Sanna did not hug her back, only stood there, inscrutable, eyes clamped on Mila. Mila felt a creeping unease.

'At last we've found you.' Their sister's voice held no celebration. It was smooth and grey-solemn as a river stone.

'We?' Pípa frowned. A moment later, another figure stepped on to the platform, and Mila gazed into the stern face of the jarl.

'Hello, Rune,' said Bretta. 'What a merry chase you have led us on.'

'We led you no chase,' said Rune. 'We didn't ask you to follow.'

'What else is a jarl to do when she discovers two of her youngest wards have disappeared with her most dangerous?'

'He's not dangerous!' protested Pípa.

'You left no word, Mila.' Sanna's accusation flashed like lightning. 'Not even the ring, like Oskar did. And you took that too.'

'I took it,' said Pípa, holding up her thumb. 'It's as much mine as it is yours.'

'I had no choice but to leave,' said Mila, pleading. 'You didn't believe that Oskar had been taken.'

'Because he hasn't!' Sanna's chest heaved. 'He is gone, Mila. Gone because he couldn't stand his life with us. A life you make so hard—'

Bretta held out her arm and Sanna fell silent, as though slapped. 'You have worried your sister nearly to death.' There was a definite threat in the woman's voice, and Mila felt the hair on her arms rise, as though she'd been plunged into an icy bath.

'How did you find us?' said Rune suspiciously. 'How

did you catch up?'

'We rode through the days and nights. Bretta saw how important it was to me that we reached you quickly.' Sanna's voice had a reverential tone that made Mila's skin crawl.

'How did your dogs manage that, Bretta?'

'Seems you're not the only one who knows their herbs, mage.' The jarl wore an almost wolfish expression, a snarl. Her body was tense as she approached, though when she saw Mila watching her, her stance loosened, shoulders rolling back.

'Come now, child. Away from the mage.'

'He's our friend,' said Mila.

'Why are you here, Mila?' said Sanna. 'I thought you said you never wanted to leave the forest?'

'I had to follow Oskar.'

'He's here? In Bovnik?'

'No.' Mila hesitated. 'He's north. In Thule. Look.'

She pointed at the horizon, but the stars had been covered by cloud and the sea was suddenly dark and quiet. There was a silence fit for a funeral.

Bretta laughed, a little too loudly. 'Thule?'

Mila ignored Bretta and spoke only to Sanna, trying to make her understand. 'I know it sounds mad—'

'Someone has been telling tales.' The dangerous edge

was back in Bretta's voice, and her eyes were fixed on a point behind Mila. On Rune. 'What nonsense have you been filling these girls' heads with, mage?'

'It's not nonsense,' said Rune. 'The Bear took them to Thule. But it's not too late to get them back.'

'Shut up,' said Bretta bluntly. 'Why should we believe you? I should have thrown you to the cold a long time ago.'

'It's the truth,' said Rune. 'Mila has seen him for what he is.'

'I have,' she said. 'I told you, Sanna: his feet didn't sink in the snow. When he spoke my name my head ached.'

'Why must you always think you're special?' spat Sanna. 'It's pathetic, that you'd believe this boy just because he tells you you're Oskar's only hope.'

'Enough,' hissed Bretta. 'We are returning you to your home. Come, now.' She reached out and took Mila's wrist in an iron grip.

'Stavgar is not my home!'

'You're wasting our time.'

'Don't you want the boys back?'

Bretta laughed hollowly as she began to drag Mila back to the stone steps. Mila tried to wrench herself away, but it was like fighting a current. A moment later, Rune was there, trying to separate them.

'Let her go!'

Bretta shoved him, and Rune grabbed her cloak to steady himself. It ripped slightly, and beneath it something glinted.

Bretta hurried to readjust her cloak, but it was too late. Mila had seen what was wrapped tight around the woman's wrist.

Gold cord.

'He has you too.' Rune's voice seemed to cause the wind to dip.

Mila looked from Bretta's face to Rune's, then pulled out one of the glowing cords from her cloak. The jarl scowled, a muscle feathering in her jaw, then she let out an unnatural shout of laughter. 'What?'

Rune took a wider stance, a more definite tone. 'You've made a pact with the Bear.'

Mila took hold of the rip in Bretta's cloak and pulled, revealing her arms. The cord laced her wrist to the elbow, tied so tight the skin nosed up through the gaps, shining with the same strange pulse as the cord in her own hand.

'What do you mean, made a pact with a bear?' Sanna's voice was sceptical.

Rune ignored her, eyes fixed on Bretta. The tendons in the jarl's neck tensed as she fixed her jaw, baring her teeth.

'Come here, Pípa,' said Mila fearfully, and Pípa edged

towards her. Mila pushed her behind her, as far away from the jarl as possible.

'That's how you knew where to find us,' said Rune. 'That's how you caught us up. Like the boy, the wolves, the eagle . . .'

Mila felt as though she were at the still point in a storm. Everything slowed down and she could hear only a roaring in her ears, the blood punching through her body. She looked down again at the cord.

'What's that?' asked Sanna.

Bretta glanced at Mila's hand, and Mila could have sworn her eyes flashed, just like the wolves'. She hurriedly looped it over her belt as Rune placed himself between the jarl and Mila, talking in a low, calming voice, as though to a wounded animal.

'I know you had no choice, Bretta. But you can fight him now. I can help you—'

Bretta howled, and was suddenly running, surging forward, straight towards Rune. The mage side-stepped her and wrenched Mila out of the way, but he was too late to save them all.

The jarl's momentum carried Pípa over the edge of the waterfall.

Sanna screamed.

'Pípa!' Mila rushed forward and threw herself on to

her belly, hands reaching uselessly as the two figures pitched down and down. Pípa must have fought because suddenly Bretta spun away from her and hit the slick, icy rock.

A moment later, Pípa plunged directly into the churning water.

A terrible, snake-like fear reared up in Mila, baring its needle-sharp teeth, but she used it to make steel of herself. She made herself deaf to Rune, her screaming sister, and stumbled to her feet.

She looked towards the waterfall. Towards the black roar and freezing mist. Towards the impossible, iced-over drop.

And jumped.

Part 3
THULE

Chapter Twenty-Two

The Golden Current

Mila had always known she was not a particularly brave person. She'd never joined Oskar, Sanna and Papa in the breaking of the frost on the river for fishing. They'd lie on the ice and smash it with rocks at its thinnest points, laughing when it cracked into warning webs beneath them, while she called caution from the banks. She never climbed trees any more. She liked her danger at a distance, preferred adventures on the lips of others. And even now, as she felt her body fly, and then fall, she did not want to look. She squeezed her eyes shut, remembered Bretta plummeting, and knew she was going to die.

Distantly, she thought she heard Sanna scream her name, but the sound was ripped away by the rush of wind and the gush of water. She felt the water begin to wet her clothes as she skimmed its fall, sensed her cloak grow heavy with it, and the wind slapping her cheeks and ripping the cap from her head.

She could not open her eyes now even if she wanted to. They were gummed together by tears and cold, and the force of her fall blurred everything even behind her lids. Her stomach felt as though she'd left it on the platform when she jumped.

She wished she'd started counting, to have some idea of how close to the bottom she was, but as soon as she thought this she felt icy water clap its hand over her feet. She realized she'd been holding her breath the whole length of the fall. Even if she survived the impact, she would not last long under the ice without air.

Mila inhaled sharply, and the next moment she was fully beneath the water. It was as shocking as a slap. Her brain itself seemed to freeze, the water rushing through her cloak so fast she might as well have been in her underclothes. She felt no hint of the current Rune had promised, only a great, crushing pressure on her shoulders and back. She forced her eyes open. Freezing water clung to her eyeballs, boring a sharp needle into her temples as she grasped about her, searching for Pípa in the mouthing blackness.

Panic, dark and cloying as oil, spread through her body. Her cloak wrapped about her arms and legs, and she struggled out of it, hoping that would help her break free of the waterfall's press, but it was hopeless. Her lungs began to ache. Bright spots appeared in the black panic. She was going to drown. And Pípa, where was she? Though she was a stronger swimmer than Mila, surely her small body would be forced even further down.

There!

Ahead through the dark water she saw a pale figure. They swam towards each other, and suddenly Pípa's hand was in hers, her other scrabbling at her waist.

Of course! Mila had nearly forgotten the first thing Rune had gifted them. She wrenched two orbs from the belt, and handed one to Pípa. They placed them in their mouths.

Mila's teeth caught on the orb and burst it, like the skin of a berry. But inside was not fruit flesh, or liquid, but air. Air that tasted like damp moss and dew. Like home, before the winter.

She sucked it down, and the effect was instantaneous. Though her head still spun, the explosions faded to distant stars. Pípa pointed downwards. Mila's eyes were wide open now, her body so numb the water felt almost warm, and she knew that this was when the cold was most dangerous – when you stopped feeling it. Where Pípa was pointing, she saw something glowing.

A thread of light, green and gold and bright as the sky fire, wove in and around the water at the bottom, playful as an otter. But other lights were joining it, the stars in her vision spreading into explosions again, her chest desperate for breath. She was going to have to inhale. It was not a choice. It was an impulse stronger than anything, even living. Even her air-starved brain understood she was not going to make it.

Pípa brought another orb up to her mouth, and this one Mila sucked, letting the air dissolve slowly through the skin into her mouth, giving her a longer breath.

They were almost at the bright current now, the gold like a seam running through water black as wet stone. They kept tight hold of each other's hands as they let the water push them to the bottom.

Finally, Mila's fingertips brushed the golden current and—

She was wrenched forward, as though caught on a hook or the tip of a wind spin, torn from Pípa's grasp. A moment later she felt her sister's hand close on her ankle.

The gold thread appeared to be a length of fast-flowing water that swallowed her whole. Her ears popped as she hurtled along, this time desperate to keep her eyes open but barely able to. All she could discern was the gold-green shimmer weaving around her. Pípa's grip felt like the only solid thing in the whole world.

Somewhere there must be rocks, but they hit nothing, only shot forward. Was this even water? It felt like wind, wind all around them, cocooning them. Perhaps somewhere above them was the river, and above that the ice, and above that the stretch of the ravine, and finally the sky, so huge and star-filled.

An image came to Mila suddenly of Rune laying his hands one over the other and telling her about realms overlapped like fish scales. Perhaps they were slipping through one realm to another. It felt impossible that her body could travel so fast, so perhaps it wasn't. Perhaps she had been pulled from herself, and it was her spirit left now in the golden light, on its way to the otherworld.

The orb of air was dissolved completely now, leaving only the lingering taste of an early forest. Mila tried to eke out the breath, but her heart was beating too fast, her fear swallowing air like fire does, sucking it bodily from her mouth.

Just as the stars punctured her vision again, as the darkness began to swallow the edges of light, the golden seam spat them out.

The light changed from a glow to a dazzle. Mila closed her eyes again as she felt her body fall. She landed hard on her back, and the breath she'd sucked in only moments before was wrenched back out. Winded, she gasped and writhed on to her side. Beneath her glove, the ground was springy like moss, and when she managed to open her eyes, she saw that that was exactly what it was. She pushed herself up, her lungs slowly filling again, and blinked around her as Pípa landed with a thump beside her.

'That was far worse than I imagined,' wheezed Mila, massaging her neck. 'And I thought I'd imagined the worst.'

'At least Rune gave us those . . .' Pípa was panting. 'What were they again?'

'Breath-skeins.' Mila hurt, an all-over ache radiating along her back and across her chest, shooting down her legs and pulsing at the back of her head. And under it all sat a different hurt: that Rune had abandoned them.

If it weren't for the pain, she would have thought she'd left her body behind in the underwater sky fire. It was as if she were in the afterlife, because Papa had always said that's what the afterlife must feel like: like coming home. And it was as if she were at home in the forest again.

Except there was no snow, no ice. Trees in green leaf spread out above them. Rune's voice floated to her. *You must find the way past winter . . .*

'Is . . . is this . . . ?' Pípa's voice was full of wonder.

Mila swallowed down a sudden lump in her throat. 'Spring.'

Chapter Twenty-Three

The Compass

Mila had forgotten it was possible for the ground to feel like this, for there to be so much green in the world. They were in a birch grove, and apart from the lack of a heart tree it felt exactly like the one she used to visit with her family all those years ago. She ran a hand over the moss, remembering how her bare feet would sink into it, remembering Mama's hand in hers . . .

There was no sign of the river that had spat them out, only a trickle of water emerging from a gap in a small cairn of rocks, placed where the heart tree should have stood. It seemed impossible that they had emerged from there. Where was Bovnik? All about them were trees. Above them, a blue sky filled with light, but no sign of the sun. It was spring, but wrong somehow. Unnatural.

'How did we get through there?' Pípa asked, eyeing the cairn, her voice sounding hollow in Mila's popped and sore ears. But as she watched, the edges of the water began to ripple, as though they were a reflection in a windswept lake. Pípa frowned and pulled at her arm, pulling her backwards, further up the hillock. They moved just in time.

The next moment, a body was thrown on to the moss below them, raven-black hair slick and stuck to her cheeks. Mila gasped and crawled forward.

'How did she—?' started Pípa, but Mila's eyes were locked on their elder sister. Not even her chest moved. She was not breathing.

'Sanna!' She moved her sister's hair away from her mouth. Her cheeks were pale, her eyes half-closed. Mila's stomach churned as she brought her ear to Sanna's chest. A faint heartbeat stirred beneath her sister's ribs, and Mila remembered the whale bones, big enough to hold up a city.

'The breath-skein!' Pípa's exclamation pierced her panic, and suddenly her little sister was scrabbling at Mila's belt for the final orb. She wrenched open Sanna's jaw and pushed it inside. Mila kept her ear on her sister's sodden winter vest, wishing the whisper into a drumbeat.

'Come on, San,' murmured Pípa, and, as if she'd heard her, Sanna's body gave a great shudder.

Then Mila took Sanna's shoulder and rolled her on to

her side, and it seemed as if she had had a whole river in her lungs, so much water came out of her mouth.

Mila rubbed her between her shoulder blades, feeling a heartbeat beneath her palm. When Sanna had stopped vomiting, Pípa threw herself at her sisters. She wrapped both of them in her little arms and squeezed them so tight Mila felt she might be the one to have trouble breathing next.

'You're hurting, Píp,' said a muffled Sanna, and their little sister's grip relaxed. 'What just happened? The water – it was gold.' Her voice was still thick with water. 'And where are we?' She sat up carefully. 'The trees – they have leaves!'

'Thule,' said Mila. 'It's where the Bear brought Oskar.'

Sanna raised her eyebrows at her. Mila raised her eyebrows back. 'Just look around, Sanna. It's spring.'

They all three looked about them. Alongside mingled wonder and fear, Mila felt the fizz of anger in her belly. The Bear had taken spring from her forest, brought it here. He had doomed them to an eternal winter, stolen her brother – and why? For what?

Sanna's arms came up. Mila flinched, but, instead of pushing or pinching her, Sanna held her almost as tightly as Pípa had done. Mila leant into the hug, inhaling the cold river smell of her, listening to her breathing, which

174

seemed to Mila the best sound ever made.

She listened for other sounds, but heard none. The forest was deathly silent. A prickle of fear went up her back. She pushed gently away and looked around. 'We need to get moving.'

'How do you know which way to go?' Sanna asked.

'The same as always,' said Pípa confidently. 'North.'

'Which is . . . ?'

Mila blinked around them. There was no sun, and anyway, she didn't know if time worked the same way on Thule. 'We can make a compass, like Papa taught us.'

Sanna stared at her. 'You remember that?'

'I wasn't that little,' said Mila, upending the pouch Rune had filled. There were three vials of brimstone, and small pots of flameberry and moonroot.

'What're those?'

'Rune gave them to us,' Mila replied, the mage's name sticking in her throat. 'We can use this for the water.' She tipped out the moonroot and held out the empty pot. 'Pípa, will you fill this?'

Pípa went to the cairn with its trickle of water while Mila sifted through the vials and pots. 'There's no needle, nothing metal.'

Sanna, who had been staring at her, rubbed her face. 'A needle, yes. I . . .' She looked down at her sopping dress. 'I have this.'

She tenderly touched Geir's brooch, then took it off, letting her cloak fall to the ground.

Mila hesitated. 'I'll have to break it.'

Sanna swallowed, then set her jaw. She gave the clasp a sudden twist, and the pin broke free. She held it out to Mila with a faint smile, though her eyes shone. 'If you're right about this, he can make me another.'

Mila took it gently and began to push the pin through the fur trim of Sanna's fallen cloak in long strokes, as if she were trying to wipe it dry. *One, two, three . . .*

Pípa brought back the pot of water and set it on the mossy surface. 'What're you—?'

'Hush, Pip,' said Sanna softly. 'You'll make her lose count.'

Once Mila reached one hundred, she carefully lowered the brooch pin into the water. It caught on the surface and slowly, strangely, began to spin – once, twice, and back on itself, until it finally settled. Mila squinted down at it, then in the direction the point was indicating, past where Pípa sat.

'That's north.'

'How—?' began Pípa.

'Currents,' said Mila, removing the pin and emptying the water. Sanna held out the broken brooch, motioning for Mila to put it in her pouch.

'Currents?'

'Like the sky fire,' said Sanna.

Pípa frowned. 'The northern lights?'

'Mmm,' said Sanna, helping Mila to gather the scattered vials. 'You know how they dance? It's actually more of a fight, between the sun's light and our air. Currents bring them crashing together. The needle must be drawn north by the same currents.'

'I didn't know that's how it worked,' said Mila, placing her hand on Sanna's. She knew how much the brooch meant to her. 'Papa said it was magic.'

'It is, of a sort.' Sanna stood up and wrung out her hair. 'We'd better get moving.'

Chapter Twenty-Four

The Familiar Forest

It was good to be walking, but the shift from deepest winter to the warmth of spring was hard to adjust to. Mila shed her clothes down to her winter vest and they all took off their woollen socks. The fur-lined boots made Mila's feet itch but at least they were not so hot any more.

'You must believe it now, Sanna,' said Mila, as Pípa ran ahead to shimmy up trees and jump down again, laughing at the leaves that dropped with her. 'In Thule, and the Bear? Now we're here?'

'I don't really have a choice, do I? I was in the golden river just like you.'

'And that Oskar was taken?' pressed Mila.

'I don't know.' Sanna's face was downturned and shadowed. 'An island of eternal spring . . . perhaps he wanted to come here.'

'Why do you keep thinking the worst of him?'

'Because!' exclaimed Sanna. 'Because of Ma—' She stopped herself and flicked a glance at Pípa, who was halfway up an oak tree. 'Because of Papa. People leave.'

'Mama had no choice,' said Mila. 'And Papa—'

'Did,' said Sanna coolly. 'People aren't always happy with small lives. Perhaps we weren't enough for Oskar.'

'He didn't think he had a small life,' said Mila hotly. 'Just because you hate us—'

'She doesn't hate us,' said Pípa dropping down as they passed beneath the oak. 'Do you?'

'Of course not. I only wish . . .' Sanna fell silent a moment, and Mila listened to their feet and skirts rustling over the mossy ground, and to the greater, all-swallowing quiet of the forest.

'The journey,' said Sanna finally. 'I was furious with you, and worried sick, but didn't it make you see, Mila? See that the world is so big and so full of wonderful things?'

'So is home,' said Mila sulkily.

Sanna's face was alight with excitement. 'Those mountains, the sunset. I'd never seen a sunset that went all the way to the horizon. I've always been hemmed in by trees. The world is so large and we live in so small a part of it.'

Mila could think of nothing to say to that. They walked on in silence under the endless trees.

'How much further?' grumbled Pípa after a while.

'Not sure, Píp. I've never been to an island of stilled spring before, have you?' teased Sanna, tucking her skirts up between her legs and tying them together, making baggy pantaloons. She looked sort of dashing, her raven-black hair now dry and slicked back off her face, but Mila would never have told her that. She ran a hand through her own curls and her fingers got snagged immediately on an egg-sized knot.

Mila felt an unpleasant sort of wakefulness, as though her eyelids were held open by matchsticks and her skin was tingling with buzzing insects. Rune had told her a little of what to expect, but still she knew nothing was certain.

Mila kept her gaze fixed on the moss beneath their feet, the itch of her winter vest a welcome distraction from her racing mind.

'There!' Pípa suddenly exclaimed, pointing. Sanna gasped. Mila raised her head. She had to blink several times to be sure of what she was seeing. Was this one of the strange things Rune had told them about on the platform? What else of what he had described would they find?

A bare hill rose in the centre of a field full of wild flowers – purple and red and blue – rippling like wheat in a breeze. They were the flowers that had bloomed around the heart tree in spring, but here they grew so thick and so high Mila felt sure they were magic. The hill looked like an island, marooned in a colourful, calm sea. It glittered white, like marble.

'What's that?' asked Sanna.

'The Bear's cave,' breathed Mila.

'Is that where Oskar is?'

Mila nodded grimly. She realized that, until now, she had forgotten to be afraid. Walking through the forest had felt comforting, like being at home, even though in Eldbjørn forest the trees were weighed with snow and the river was caught under a pane of ice, thumb thick. Here, walking through a spring forest, it was easy to forget that this island was not on any map. Now Mila looked behind and the trees seemed to be straining after them.

'Come on,' she said, moving clear of the treeline and into the field of wild flowers. The sisters stepped forward.

When they'd viewed it from the forest, the cave had seemed no more than half a mile from the trees, but every time Mila stood on tiptoe to see over the head-high grass and flowers, it was as though it had drifted slightly further away, like a lazily tethered cloud. The scent of the wild flowers was overpowering, and all she wanted to do was lie down amid the whispering grasses and sleep. She imagined Oskar approaching the cave. Had he been afraid, or so deep under the Bear's spell he had not felt or seen anything? She did not know which would be worse: fear, or oblivion.

Eventually the cave loomed up over them, and she felt a dizzying sense that it might topple and fall down, smashing them to pieces. She shuddered, and tried to calm her hammering heart, which was throwing itself at her ribs like a caged bird.

The flowers grew up to a line of low black stones, beyond which was a raked stone path and the curve of the cave. Mila stopped at the boundary. Maybe the stones would turn into a thousand scuttling crabs and nip them to pieces, or the path would suck them in like sinking sand.

Pípa had no such worries. She crossed the line as if it were nothing.

'Come on,' she said impatiently. Mila and Sanna followed. The wall of the cave was dazzling up close, and Mila shaded her eyes. It seemed smooth and impenetrable, without weakness.

'How do we get through?' said Sanna.

Mila closed the distance between them and wall, and after a moment's hesitation held out her hand and placed it gently on the rock. She had the strangest sensation that if she pushed hard enough, she could push all the way through. Like dough.

What had Rune said when she first met him? Something about feeling with more than her fingers, seeing with more than her eyes . . .

'Come,' she said to her sisters. 'We have to push through.'

Sanna snorted. 'That's impossible.'

'Isn't this all impossible?' snapped Mila. Her head was starting to throb, her legs to ache. And all the time, time was rushing by. Oskar was moving closer to . . . Not death. What Rune had told her was almost worse.

She forced herself to speak calmly. 'Please, Sanna. Try to see. Try to feel. It's not rock at all. Watch.'

Mila closed her eyes and took a shaky breath, repeating Rune's words: *There are things in the world that you have to look at with more than your eyes, hear with more than your ears, touch with more than your fingers.*

She had seen the Bear stand on soft snow and not sink. She had seen a boy bound by the ice, watched wolves and an eagle and a jarl attack them. She had seen her brother's face become that of another.

She had seen all these things, and now she knew she could see the wall for what it was. Dough, it felt like, and dough it would become.

Mila pressed softly. She was in the kitchen with Sanna, watching her plunge her fingers into the flour sack and bring them up with a flourish, scattering a thin dusting on the wood of their table, the table where they carved their given names into its soft underside. She held a cup of fresh-melted snow, and watched her sister scoop a double handful of flour on to the dusted tabletop, sift it through her fingers and form it into a mound. She made a hollow with her thumb and nodded, and Mila began to pour the water into the hollow, a little at a time, pausing for Sanna to work the water into the flour.

'What're you doing?'

Pípa's voice came as a shock in the quiet of Mila's mind kitchen, but Sanna shushed their little sister and soon Mila was back, watching as the flour and water performed their small alchemy. When the dough was formed, it was Mila's job to leave it by the fire to rise, and she imagined reaching down to press her palm into it. The dough was warm and flour-dusted, firm but not solid. She pushed a little harder, feeling it give, taking her hand in, pushing up between her fingers.

'How are you doing that?' There was wonder in Sanna's voice, and Mila, careful not to lose the sensation of the dough, opened her eyes.

Her hand was embedded in the wall.

Mila's heart began to beat faster, and she swallowed down the panic that instantly rose at the strangeness of it. Because she was seeing what she was feeling: the wall was less solid now, the marble turned to glittering ice crystals held in a cloud, and she was pushing through it.

'How—?'

'Shush, Pípa!'

Trying to ignore her sisters, Mila focused on the movement of her hand, sinking deeper until she was in past her wrist. She allowed herself to breathe more regularly, and brought her other hand up, pressing it alongside until she was up to her elbows and her nose was touching the – what?

Mila stopped, breathing so close and hot a small hollow was forming at her lips, melting the wall and sending water trickling down her arms.

'Is that snow?'

This time Pípa shushed Sanna, and Mila saw and felt that that was exactly what it was. It was an enormous bank of snow, swept up high as a hill. It did not make sense: the blue sky still shone with sunless light, behind them the field of flowers waved their heads lazily. But she was up to her shoulders in snow. Her arms began to burn with the cold shock of it.

'Are your hands through?'

Mila shook her head. It was thicker than her arm's reach.

'What do I do?' she said in a small voice, and Sanna came to stand beside her.

'We will all push through at the same time. Run, and keep on running. Whatever's there.'

Mila felt a small match of hope strike in her thudding chest. Sanna, finally, seemed to be on her side.

'Ready?' Pípa and Mila nodded. It felt good to let their big sister boss them around. 'Three, two, one!'

Mila took the step that would take her inside the snow. The sounds of her sisters disappeared, muffled to silence. It was like being back in the snow crush, but this time she had solid ground beneath her feet.

Using her arms as paddles, she swept the snow apart, straining her legs against the compacting, trying not to listen to the creak and pop that meant the balance of the wall was shifting above them. It was strange how much it sounded like wood in a fire.

After five tortuous strides, her hands stopped touching snow and instead found air. Mila leant forward, using her elbows to draw herself out of the bank, and tumbled face first, down into the Bear's cave.

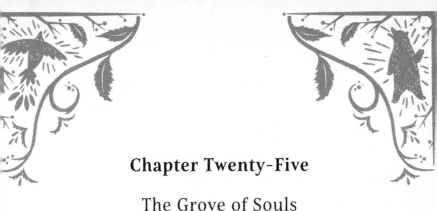

Chapter Twenty-Five

The Grove of Souls

Inside was dark as dirt, dark as a mouth. The hole they'd made was high above them, leaking meagre light, the slope of the ground cushioning her fall. Mila heard Pípa and Sanna collapse beside her, and instantly groped for their hands, holding them tightly in the blackness. She stretched her eyes as wide as she could, the sudden cold of the cave making them water.

Mila knelt, still holding her sisters' hands, shuffling them closer together. She could hear only their three sets of shallow, fearful breaths, feel only the blunt shunt of darkness pressing in. Beneath her knees was what smelt like the bitter richness of earth.

She unfurled her hand from Sanna, who let out a small mew of fear, and reached down to touch the ground. It was dirt, but mixed with something. Mila shuddered as her hand traced a gnarled shape.

Wood – roots twisting across the floor. She sensed

Pípa and Sanna also reaching down, and felt a sudden heat at her side. She thrust her hand into her cloak, knowing already what she would find . . .

The two pieces of cord shining gold, as hot as sunbeams in her hand. She gathered up her cloak to hold them.

'What're they?' whispered Sanna, her voice terribly loud in the yawning silence, her face lit by the eerie golden glow.

'His,' replied Mila. 'They're what he uses to bind the boys.'

'Why do you have them?' hissed Sanna, looking as though they were snakes coiled to strike. Mila could not bear to recount the story of the second piece.

'Found them.'

'At least we have a light,' said Pípa.

There was only one way to go. The tunnel yawned before them, roots catching the paltry light, paving the path ahead. Towards Oskar. Towards the Bear.

Heart thrumming in her chest, palms sweating, Mila took a step, and then another. She paused between each one, listening. But the earth muffled their steps so well that, had she not looked back at regular intervals to make sure they were still together, she might have thought herself alone. Pípa's face was drawn in the thin light, and

Sanna walked beside her in her torn and ragged skirts, biting her lip.

The tunnel seemed to stretch for ever, the light and heat from the gold cords growing stronger and stronger, until eventually Mila saw a flickering ahead, as though from a fire. She froze, her sisters huddling together beside her.

'Come on, Milenka,' murmured Sanna. 'Oskar's waiting.'

They hugged the shadows of the black walls, and approached the light. The ground dropped suddenly away. Sanna flung out an arm to stop Pípa charging ahead. Before them was a cavernous space, reaching as deep below them as it did high above. And at its centre was the most fantastical thing Mila had ever seen.

'What . . . ?' breathed Sanna.

Mila swallowed. 'His heart tree.'

It was at least ten times bigger than the one in Eld-bjørn forest. It arrowed up before them, its base a tangle of body-thick roots, its trunk so colossal ten people with their arms outstretched could not have encompassed it. And growing from its massive branches were leaves as large as sails. They were gold, like the cords in her hand, and cast everything in a flame-like light, stronger even than the torches ranged about the room, though no sun shone down on it. The light seemed to come from inside the tree itself.

Mila could see no sign of the huge, broad figure of the Bear. But what she could see was almost as awful.

There were dozens, perhaps hundreds, of smaller shadows: tiny trees twisted into bizarre shapes, leaning towards the birch at their centre. Each was bound with gold cord that then snaked its way to the base of the heart tree, disappearing into the snarl of roots.

It may have been the glitter of the tree and torches, casting everything in a tricksy glow, but the cord almost looked as though it was pulsing. Even the pieces of cord in Mila's hand seemed to twitch. She shuddered and pushed them back into her cloak.

'What are we waiting for?' said Sanna, suddenly bold. 'Where's Oskar? We need to find him.'

Mila felt sick as she remembered what Rune had told her at the top of Bovnik's waterfall. It had felt so impossible she'd hardly believed it. But now she had to tell her sister where – or rather what – Oskar was.

'He's somewhere there,' said Pípa weakly, stretching out a trembling finger. 'That's right, isn't it, Mila? That's what Rune said.'

Sanna squinted at where Pípa was pointing. 'Behind the trees?'

Mila shook her head carefully, her gut churning. 'They *are* the trees.'

Sanna could have been turned to ice, she froze so completely. Only her lips moved, trembling. 'You . . . you mean . . . ?'

Mila took her sister's hand. She spoke as clearly and calmly as she could, trying to recall what Rune told them: 'He plants them, to feed his heart tree. See how some are more boy than tree?'

Sanna peered more closely at the shapes. Mila tried not to look, but she had already seen – how some were only rooted about their ankles by gold cord, swaying as though in a breeze. Others were so enveloped in bark that she would not have known them from trees.

'Oskar – is he . . . what if he's . . . ?'

'That's why Rune brought us so quickly,' said Mila. 'So we could still get him out.'

They looked down at the grove of planted boys, at the heart tree rooted at their centre. Mila wanted to weep, looking at the caught shapes.

'Can't we help them all?' asked Pípa but sadly, as though she already knew the answer.

Sanna shook her head. 'We're here for Oskar. We can't risk being seen.'

Mila knew what it cost her to say that. Geir was

down there too.

'Then let's go,' said Pípa. Before either of them could stop her, she darted towards the steps that led down into the cavern. Sanna followed close, and, after a brief pause, Mila hauled her courage into her chest, and descended.

A few of the shapes that were more boy than tree looked up, but their movements were lackadaisical, like animals emerging from hibernation. Where was the Bear? In the snarl of roots? In the glittering leaves above? The idea that he might be watching them was almost worse than being certain of it.

At the base of the steps, Mila gestured for Sanna and Pípa to go right, and she circled left, trying to avoid touching any trees. *Anyone*, she corrected herself.

The shimmering light of the golden-leafed tree made them seem gilded: living statues meant to decorate the cave of the Bear. She tried not to think of them as people – as brothers or sons with homes and lives that might continue if they helped them.

Mila jumped. She felt breath on her cheek. A boy was speaking close to her ear, eyes unfocused.

'I'm sorry—' she began, but he wasn't looking at her, or talking to her, but to something in the distance.

She hoped that, whatever the Bear did to keep them –

how had Rune put it? – sunk into themselves, he allowed them to think happy things. Though, having met him, Mila doubted it. She backed away, bumping into another boy. She turned to him, and gasped.

Chapter Twenty-Six

The Rooted Boys

It was Geir, reddish hair burnished to copper in the tree light, his cheeks sallow, his jaw slack. His hands hung limp at his sides, and his feet were bound with gold, sunk inches into the dirt.

Mila's throat tightened. She reached out and grasped his hand. It was rigid and rough as bark.

'Geir?'

The boy did not move and his expression did not change, but his eyes dragged themselves away from the middle distance to Mila's face. She swallowed and moved a little closer.

'Geir?'

His eyes looked like two black tunnels, their faded light growing sharper the longer he looked at her. She fumbled in Rune's pouch and drew out the brooch he had made Sanna. *Something he loved.* She held the two pieces up to his face, hesitated a moment, then placed the

194

piece of elk horn in Geir's hand. The boy's fingers twitched, then brushed over the carved brooch. Mila held her breath, watching his face. Something slid behind his gaze.

Mila could not think what it was, but it was something alive, similar to the shadow she had seen in Oskar's face the night he'd been taken, only where that had been dark and eel-like, this was light.

Geir was coming back to himself.

A vein in his forehead began to pulse, and his eyes grew wide even as the light returned to them.

'Help me!' he gasped.

Fear was growing in his eyes, sucking his cheeks pale, filling his lungs with a scream that Mila did her best to smother.

'Hush!' she whispered desperately, holding her hand over his mouth. 'Hush! He'll hear!'

But she saw now she had made a terrible mistake. She had reminded Geir of who he was, and where he was. He pawed weakly at her hand on his mouth and seemed unable to move fast, but she could see his mind was racing.

'Geir,' she said quietly, as though talking to Dusha when she was frightened. 'It's all right, Geir. I'm here, and so are Pípa and Sanna and—'

At the mention of Sanna's name, Geir's eyes widened. He looked desolate, desperate tears streaking down his cheeks. Mila carried on talking, as gently and soothingly as she could, all the while looking about her for the Bear. Would he be able to tell one of his prisoners had been woken?

'I had to break the brooch, you see? She'll be angry, so I need to return it to her mended. You can mend it, can't you? But you have to calm down, Geir. You have to promise not to make a sound. Do you understand me?'

She looked him in the eyes, and he saw her. He took two deep breaths through his nose, and Mila pulled her hands from his lips.

She knelt and looked for knots in the cord, but there were none. It seemed to loop in one continuous, un-broken length from ankle to knee. She would have to cut it. Mila pulled Oskar's knife from her belt. Holding her breath, she worked it beneath the cord, and sliced upwards.

The cord would not break. Mila tried again and again, but she could not cut it. The cord seemed to be made of something harder than metal. 'I'm sorry, I can't—'

But Geir was not listening. He seemed frozen, looking behind her. Mila wheeled around, coiling her body, ready to run, or attack, but it was not the Bear.

Sanna stood there, eyes filling with tears. She stumbled forward, and Mila looked away as Sanna and Geir embraced. A moment later Sanna turned back to her. 'We found him,' she whispered.

A shot of energy pierced Mila's body.

'Where?'

Sanna pointed. 'I'll stay with Geir.'

Mila hurried through the grove, casting a look at the heart tree, her breath hitching as she thought she saw a movement in the uppermost branches, but perhaps it was only the golden leaves glinting. Ahead, Pípa came into sight, crouched next to a familiar figure.

Oskar.

Pípa was pulling at his cords, her shoulders shaking. Mila ran faster and at last looked into her brother's face.

He was thin and horribly pale, his eyes, more black than brown, empty and staring. But he was there. He was alive. Mila felt winded. She wanted to throw her arms around him and never let go.

'I can't untie it!' Pípa cried.

Mila could see her hands were blistered, and that the golden cord seemed to be tightening even as she continued to pull on it. She had removed Papa's ring: Mila could see where the heated band had burnt a welt about the base of Pípa's thumb.

Mila pulled her sore hands gently away. She once again tried to use Oskar's knife to slice through the cord, but it would not break. She hissed in frustration, then remembered how Geir's face had changed when she'd placed the brooch in his hands. *Something he used and loved.* She pressed the knife against Oskar's unmoving palm.

Oskar's eyes began to warm. He came up slower than Geir, less fearful, and she watched his mouth slip into the shape of her name. 'Mila?'

'Oskar.'

She at last held her brother again, beneath this monstrous tree at the end of the world. A smaller set of arms wrapped around her, and she felt Pípa nestle in beside them. The thunder of her heartbeat finally started to calm as Oskar hugged them back.

They let go. His face was still pale, but his eyes were bright with tears. 'How . . . ?'

'There's no time,' she said, looking about them. 'We have to get you free.'

'We brought your ring, Oskar,' said Pípa, handing it to him as Mila knelt by his feet, trying to find a break in the cord. 'I looked after it for you.'

'You should keep it.'

Pípa gingerly touched her burnt thumb, looking at

the ring with distaste. 'I think Mila should have it. She's the one who made us come after you.'

Mila jumped as Oskar gently slid the ring on to her middle finger. His hand, no longer stiff and dead-feeling, reached out and brushed her cheek.

The gentleness made her feel every hurt in her body: from her sore legs to her bruised ribs, her aching feet and cord-burnt hands. She wanted to let him lift her, as Papa used to, and carry her home.

But there was still so far to go. They had not yet learnt how to break the cord. Rune must have thought Oskar's knife would be enough. If he was wrong about that, what else was he wrong about?

Even as this thought reverberated in her head, Oskar's careful touch tightened and then she was pulled from his grasp. He grabbed at her but she was caught beneath the armpits and, in a horrible fulfilment of her wish, was lifted as though she were small again and her father were scooping her on to his shoulders. But there were no hands beneath her, only her brother's panicked face and an awful expanse of cold wind that raised her high off the ground, and spun her to face the tree.

Chapter Twenty-Seven

Caught

From the snarl of dark at the mighty birch's roots came a figure. It was huge and shaped like a bear, but formed of . . . nothing. Where it should have had boundaries there were rips in the fabric of the air, swallowing light. Limbs flickered in and out of being, like shadows only just remembering to hold their form. A smell like bitter, rotting leaves clawed up Mila's nose, thick and biting as fanged smoke.

Her stomach filled with bile. She wanted to look away, but her eyelids were pinned open by the wind that was lifting her. Her ears popped, as though she had been submerged deep into the golden current of the waterfall again, when she heard his voice.

'You dare to come uninvited to my home? To try to steal my souls and destroy my new forest?' Mila was being held at his eye-height, many feet off the ground, and he was solidifying, forming into a bear with thick, shaggy fur and burning golden eyes. Over one mighty, rolling shoulder, Mila saw the glint of his axe.

She felt a click in her throat, as if it had been released from a tightening noose, and her voice garbled out, pulled like a magician drawing silks from a hat.

'You came uninvited to our home. Stole our brother.' She did not want to speak, but she felt she had no choice. She was conscious of her words but somehow unable to control them.

He was really solid now, huge and stinking of forest rot. But though his paws were wide as tree trunks, his body mighty as a boat's hull, he drifted through the boy-trees with smoke-like ease. They seemed to shudder and bend away from him, cringing as though caught in a fierce wind. His eyes fixed her in his awful, animal gaze. 'Ah, yes. Little Mila.'

She cried out as his voice bore sharply into her head.

'You saw me without my cords.'

Mila remembered his unbound feet, hovering above soft snow. They were unbound now too. The cord must contain his magic, bind him fully into his human form, just as it bound the boys' will to his own.

'Very careless of me,' hiss-roared the Bear. 'But girls are often disarming. That's why I usually do not bother with them.' The Bear's face twisted in a dreadful smile, yellow teeth showing in the swallowing dark of his face. 'But I can make an exception.'

Below her, she saw a flash of ragged blue dress. She tried to stop herself looking down but it was too late – the golden eyes followed her gaze, and a slow terror filled Mila's body as his jaw opened again, another baring of teeth cracking the black fur of his face.

'I almost forgot there were more of you. Do we have the complete set? Sanna, wasn't it?' Mila heard a thin keen of pain from her sister, and felt another rush of cold wind as Sanna was wrenched from her hiding place and brought to hover beside Mila. She tried to reach out to comfort her, but her arms were trapped against her sides.

'And is Pípa here too?'

Mila's breath hitched as she fought the impulse to answer him. There was silence.

'Pípaaaa,' he crooned, but all was still and quiet. Mila's mind raced. She had to keep him talking.

'Why do you take the boys?' she cried. 'Why did you send the winter?'

He stopped casting around the grove and fixed her in his golden gaze. 'Who told you I sent the winter?'

Again, Mila's mouth turned traitorous. 'Rune!'

The glinting eyes flashed in recognition. 'The mage.

I've heard of him. Never could find him, though.'

'Well?' she said, more bravely than she felt. 'Why did you take them? Why did you bring the winter? You have ruined lives, you're killing my home—'

The Bear stood on his hind legs, bringing him tall as a tree, and roared. The sound slammed through her body as Mila felt the supporting wind ripped from under her. She landed hard on her back at Oskar's rooted feet, and he cried, 'Mila!' Beside her, Sanna landed too, moaning in pain and reaching out for her, trying to shield her. Pípa was still nowhere to be seen.

The Bear bounded forward, threw Sanna aside with one massive shoulder and bore down on Mila, filling her vision until his awful face was all she could see, his reeking breath all she could feel, his words all she could hear.

'*Your* home?' he spat in his howling voice, with such force the boy-trees around them shook and Mila's hair blew off her face. 'Eldbjørn was never your home. It was mine. Humans brought nothing, planted nothing, and took everything.' His eyes were wild, wide, hurt. 'I punish those who threaten that most sacred place.'

Her heart quaking in her chest, his body bearing down like a wave upon her, Mila remembered the heart tree lying dead and broken on the forest floor.

The Bear gave a snarl and threw himself off her, sank back on his haunches, the blade of his woodcutter's axe sliding about in its harness, toy-small on his bulk.

'Five years ago, that man chopped my heart tree to pieces like it was nothing. He tried to kill me, kill my forest. So I brought what I could save of the heart tree to Thule. I planted it here, so it would always be safe and strong.' He looked up at the birch, the vertiginous trunk making Mila's head spin.

'Someone chopped down your tree?' Mila said. 'Why? Who?'

'I never cared to ask.' The Bear's gold eyes glinted at the trunk. 'But I planted him the deepest.'

Mila gasped. About halfway up was a shape, larger than most of the others, twisted with bark but still recognizably a man, melded with the massive trunk and held so thickly with golden cord it was like a fly had been wrapped by a giant spider. The hurt in the Bear's eyes hardened into fury.

'He tried to kill my heart tree, so I made him the new heart. I keep this tree strong with the very people who would make my forest weak. I feed it on souls and spring, and I will take every boy of Eldbjørn and keep endless winter there until you are all dead or gone. Then I will return to *my* home, and bring spring with me to the

204

forest once more.'

Mila saw his fur begin to bristle. His anger was barely in check: soon he would lose control entirely. She hurried to say something, anything, to calm him.

'That's a terrible thing, a cruel thing,' she said, as soothingly as she could with her voice shaking in her throat. 'But why have you done something so cruel and terrible in return? Why punish boys for a man's crime?'

The Bear looked at her. His eyes were wary as a fox's in a trap. 'Because boys grow into men. Because without men in the forest – a forest of eternal winter – in time there will be no more people. Soon I will have driven every – last – one – of – you – out.' He pounded the ground with each word.

Mila's teeth rattled, and she was thrown back against Oskar's legs. It was a shock to feel him behind her, still rooted in place.

'Now, Mila. Didn't I say I always welcome those who come, tired, to my door?' The Bear reached down, to where the roots were shining golden at his paws. He brought his axe to the root, hooked the edge of the blade through it, and pulled.

Mila gasped as the root began to stretch, lengthening like it was not wood at all, but something pliable, like dough. *Like half-dried sap*, she thought, remembering the mess of the frozen heart tree, honey-red sap caught like blood falling from a wound. He stretched it until he had a length the height of him, then sliced it into two pieces with his axe.

The Bear crouched over the place he had pulled it from, which was ragged and pulsing, and placed a huge paw over it. His golden eyes closed a moment, and Mila saw him slump slightly. His paw was light on the root, almost tender. When he took it away again, the root was smooth, running in an unblemished twist to the trunk of the massive heart tree. He had healed it.

The tenderness vanished quick as a finger snap when he looked up again. 'Enough for you both,' he said, in a smile-snarl of a voice. 'Mila, Sanna. Bind yourselves.'

He threw the cords down, and to her horror Mila's first reaction was to reach for a piece. Her shoulder nearly wrenched out of its socket in her haste to pick it up. Sanna's arm shot forward too as his words repeated themselves in her head, so loudly it crowded out her own thoughts. *Bind yourself. Bind yourself.* Mila tried to resist, felt Sanna struggling beside her.

'Now, girls,' came the Bear's voice, warningly. 'If you fight, I will break your mind. You'll die not knowing who you are, that you were ever loved, without a memory in your head.'

Mila fought her grasping hands. *Bind yourself.* Her will broke, and his voice rushed in.

And so did Pípa.

Chapter Twenty-Eight

The Heart Tree's Heart

It happened in a moment. Pípa's small, swift shape leapt from the shadows of a nearby tree, through the air and on to the Bear's back. Mila saw her land lightly on his shoulder. He turned his massive head, and at the same time, the Bear's voice in Mila's head broke off.

Sanna threw down her cord and tore Mila's piece from her hands. The Bear let out another roar, reaching to his shoulder for his axe—

But Pípa was too quick. All her practice climbing trees on even the most blustering winter nights had given her a grip of steel, and she already had the axe in her grasp. She shimmied off the Bear, darting towards her sisters.

'Come here, Pípa—' he snarled, reaching for her, but Pípa did not so much as wince. He had no power over her. *Of course!* thought Mila. *She doesn't have her given name!*

The Bear's form began to shift and ripple. He was

turning into a spirit again. Once he did, there would be no trapping him. Through the fog of her panic Mila remembered bound legs sinking into snow . . .

She unfroze. 'Wrap his legs!' she yelled at Sanna, who picked up the fallen cords. They ran forward together, Mila yanking the other pieces from her cloak and leaping up to bind the arm that swiped at Pípa. She caught it and brought the ends of the cord together. Instantly they sealed, tightening around the Bear's arm as Sanna trapped his legs.

The Bear howled and keeled forward like a felled tree. He was bound on both arms and both legs, his shape shrinking and sharpening its edges, back into a man, the stranger who had come to their door all those nights ago. Mila threw herself clear and Oskar dragged her to her feet.

Though he was trapped in his man's form, the Bear was still as unrelenting and deadly as a snow crush. He pulled himself up and forward, towards Sanna, who was brandishing Oskar's knife.

'His axe!' cried Mila. 'Give me his axe!'

She watched the glinting arc of it fly from Pípa's hand to hers, felt an awful, tearing pain as the blade grazed her palm. Her mind went numb, not letting her feel the damage as she fumbled for the handle, already slippery with blood, transferring it to her other hand. It felt familiar in her grasp. Now, she was certain.

'You're hurt,' started Oskar, but she did not listen, only sliced through his bindings, turned from him, and began to run.

The Bear's words were like wolves, snapping at her heels. *Five years ago, that man chopped my heart tree to pieces.*

Five years . . .

Mila fixed her gaze on the bulge in the trunk and ran towards it, ignoring the fire of her injured hand. At the base of the tree she tucked the axe into her belt, ripped a section of her skirt with her teeth and, trying to look only out of the corner of her eye, she wrapped it twice around her injured hand. It would not stop the pain, but at least it might stop the bleeding.

At least now she could climb.

Mila looked at the shape sealed against the tree. It was higher than Mila had ever climbed, even before Papa had left and she'd stopped climbing trees. It was a good thirty feet before the lowermost branches began.

You mustn't think of it like that, said Mama's voice. *It's only one hand after another, until you reach the top. One hand at a time.*

Mila dropped her gaze, scanned the bark, and found

her first foothold. The trunk was oddly warm. It reminded her of the cord, its vague pulse. She placed one foot into a twist of root, and pushed herself up. She reached with her injured hand, biting down hard on her lip, letting the pain rush over her. *One hand after another.* Mila began to climb.

The rhythm of her reaching, pulling, pushing, matched the sickening twin pulse of her heart and hand. Her limbs felt like lead, her skin raw, but she would not let go.

She heard the Bear snarl. 'Mila!' He began to run towards the tree, cord shining around his limbs.

He was fast, but Mila knew she could be faster. She would reach the heart tree's heart. And she would rip it out.

Her anger propelled her better than fear. Before she knew it, she was hauling herself on to the branch below the bulge webbed in gold, and instantly began to slice the axe through cord after cord, letting them shrivel and fall.

At last the bare expanse of the tree's bulging bark was revealed. Without hesitating, Mila plunged the axe into it. She heaved it downwards with both hands, her injured palm aflame with pain. The bark was thick as sea ice, but it gave beneath the blade. Once it was split, she tore great hunks of it away and pressed her hand against the wood beneath.

It was pale and pulpy, softened and ringed with years. But there, that was a chest, a man's chest, dressed in a brown tunic. And that was a hand, snarled into woody knots, but a hand still. And here was a face, eyes black whorls of wood, a face she knew . . .

The pain in her hand, the roaring of the Bear: it all dropped away.

'Papa.'

Mila stared, wondering, at her father's carven face. It felt as though she were underwater, her body moving through thick currents, dragging her down. She brought the ring up to the gnarled hand, and slipped it over one wooden finger.

Nothing happened. Mila pressed the ring harder against the tree, holding it in place as she leant her forehead on her father's still chest. Was that a flutter, faint as a moth throwing itself against an ice window? Tears came streaming hot down her cheeks as she cradled her cut hand and whispered, 'Come back, Papa. Come back.'

The pain was all that answered. It bit and stung and throbbed, wrapping her whole arm in thorns. She had been so sure she was right, so sure it would work.

Beneath her clutching hand, the ringed finger twitched. *Boom. Boom. Boom.*

A far-off knocking in her ear, growing louder and louder until finally, the chest beneath her head heaved. Mila's father blinked his eyes, now ice blue, then keeled forward.

Mila could not think what to do but hold on. They were hurtling down, her father as limp as a corpse. With a sickening thud, they hit a branch that broke their fall, Mila shielded from the worst of the impact by her father's body.

He let out a cry of pain, but to Mila it was as wonderful as a laugh.

'Papa!' she flung her arms over him.

'Mila?' his voice was wheezy and as dry as firewood. His eyes fluttered open, struggled to focus. 'My Milenka?'

'Give me back my heart, Mila.' The Bear stood on a branch above them. Terror gripped Mila's throat as her name in his mouth sent pain grinding through her skull. The Bear was panting, his fingernails torn and bleeding. His golden eyes flashed. Mila stood between him and her father.

'And drop the axe,' he hissed, pointing with his bound arm. 'Or I will throw you off this tree.'

Mila moved the axe – her father's axe – behind her back, even as her mind urged her to hand it over. The

213

pain in her palm was becoming stronger, stinging like a hundred bees. She could see the cord glowing around the Bear's limbs, forming an unbroken circle. He was trapped fully in his human form, but he was still as dangerous as a caged animal.

Mila shook her head, the coin taste of fear rising as her hand pulsed. She dared not look at it.

'Very well,' he snarled, coiling himself to leap, when the heart tree gave a yawning creak. Mila and the Bear both looked up at the place where Mila had carved her father out of the trunk.

The tree creaked again, then swayed. Suddenly, with an awesome *crack*, the trunk split above their heads, and the entire canopy began to tip downwards.

The Bear roared, and it was the saddest, most frightening sound Mila had ever heard. It was pain and anger and fear, all mixed together into one mighty sound that filled her whole body.

Her world tilted as her father threw her over his shoulder and swung himself down on to the tree's trunk. She could barely believe he was real, but here he was, holding her, his body warm and his grip fierce.

'Hold on, Milenka!'

The Bear fell silent. He seemed shocked into stillness, could only watch as his heart tree came tilting, almost slowly, lazily, towards the ground. Mila lost sight of him as her father scaled down. But she could not lose sight of what was happening to the tree, or what was coming from it.

The bark was blackening, as if it were smouldering, and the whole cavern was filling with light. When Mila felt heat, she knew it must be fire . . . but she could smell no smoke, hear no crackling flames.

Instead, a mossy, green scent was filling her nostrils. A scent she had almost forgotten before they had arrived in Thule, but now remembered as birds in trees, and flowers underfoot. It was the smell of the whole world stretching itself awake.

It smelt like spring.

Mila's hand was hurting badly, a nauseating, rhythmic stabbing that came in time with her heartbeat. She felt herself fading as she hugged it to her, keeping a tight hold on her father's tunic with the other. Her fingers found the darned patch that Mama had mended, sitting beside the kitchen fire. Mila had been no more than four, had played with the dangling thread. She heard her mother, round with Pípa, laughing . . .

And now she could hear Sanna crying 'Papa!' and Oskar saying 'Run!' and more shattering creaks, and the smell of spring was growing stronger and stronger.

All around them were moans and cries, and Mila saw the grove was swaying, as though caught in a breeze. The golden cords were fading, turning black, like the bark of the heart tree. It was dying, and the Bear's power was dying with it. The boys were waking, remembering themselves, struggling free of the charred bark, branches reforming into limbs and chests and terrified faces.

Mila thought she felt rain, but, looking up, she saw the snow dome of the cave was melting as the freed spring bathed everything in a light so bright it clawed at her eyes.

She shut them again, and felt Oskar take her in his arms, and, through half-closed lids, saw Papa being supported by the newly freed Geir and Sanna, Pípa running alongside. The whole cave was shaking as the tree gave up its roots.

But where is the Bear?

'It's going to come down on our heads,' yelled Oskar to the waking boys. 'Get out! Run!'

Now, Mila smelt burning. It felt so out of place she did not instantly understand, but when she turned towards the felled tree she saw a dazzling brightness as the released spring sun caught the dead trunk in its jaws and began to devour it, flames leaping faster and higher with each passing second.

'Hurry!' shouted Pípa, and they followed her, up the steps and into the burning air, a girl too young still for her given name, yet she was like a jarl leading her troops to battle.

Oskar set Mila down gently, panting hard, supporting her as best he could, though he swayed with weakness.

Mila looked around. She could see no trace of the forest they had walked through. The field of wild flowers was fading before their eyes, replaced by land that was barren and dead-looking, and Mila could see the sea quite close – the island had become far smaller than when they had crossed it to find the Bear's cave. Spring had been released, and Thule seemed to be dying.

Or maybe it was just showing its true form, how it had been before the Bear came.

Beyond the island's edge, beyond the sea caught beneath its winter ice, was land: Bovnik, with its shining slice of thawing waterfall.

But now there was a new danger. A crack like a whip sounded from somewhere beyond Mila's blurry field of vision and Sanna gasped.

'The ice!' she shouted. 'It's melting!'

Chapter Twenty-Nine

Across the Frozen Sea

Oskar hauled Mila into a run. Every breath in Mila's chest was like a vice being screwed tighter and tighter, allowing less and less air, but she kept her eyes on Oskar, and on her father just ahead of her, as they ran for their lives.

She was beyond feeling cold or warmth, beyond feeling anything but the pain scraping through her ribs, her lungs, and most of all her hand. She looked down briefly and saw scarlet striping her palm, more red in the melting snow, like a spray of poppies. Her head spun.

Oskar was speaking to her, saying words that were as incomprehensible as wind, as soothing as warm water. Papa dropped back to run beside her with Sanna and Geir. She looked into his face, his blue eyes wide with concern. Behind them was the column of smoke that was swallowing the Bear's tree. She thought she saw something vast and dark moving towards them. Something running.

Papa picked her up again as she faded in and out, at times blinded by black, at others by light, riding the swell and fall, the red edge of pain that ate up her arm, through to her bones, formed a fog around her brain. *It's like cold*, she thought. Like being caught out in a snow storm, or buried in that snow crush. It was so entire it was all there was, spreading out to the very edges of her being.

'Mila,' Oskar said, like a prayer, or a wish. 'Mila. Mila.'

She was pulled back again as her father set her gently on the ground.

'I can't carry her across there,' she heard him say. 'We need to spread out.'

'There's no time!' came Geir's panicked voice.

Mila forced her heavy lids open as she felt Oskar brace his arm under her, taking her weight. They stood at the island's edge, and ahead, blue-white and broad as the sky, stretched the frozen sea. Boys were already running reck-lessly on to the ice.

But the sea would not stay frozen. Web lines of bubbles were rushing through cracks, hair thin for now, but quickly releasing in the sunlight, pushing out. She thought she could almost hear the sea breathing, sighing as it stretched its caught body, finally flexing free of winter's grip.

'Why won't it stop bleeding?' said Pípa's voice beside her.

Fluttering in the corner of her vision were anxious hands and pale faces, and she looked dully down. Pípa and Sanna were moving her arm, but she could not believe that it was her hand they touched, looking for the best point to bind it. She could barely believe that thing was a hand. It was purple and black and red as a thunderstorm viewed through closed lids, the white bone nosing up like lightning—

No.

She looked away. It was better to keep her balance, keep her grip. She leant into her father. Her papa. *Alive.*

He was solid beneath her arms, his breath steady and strong. He was here. He was real, but she could feel herself fading, becoming less, blood seeming to drain the wrong way, drain upwards, away from her legs . . .

She frowned and looked down. Her legs did look less there. And they felt less there too, numbing as though submerged in a snow drift. It seemed that, without the winter ice to keep it in place, Thule was melting from their realm, and they would vanish with it.

'Go,' she whispered.

'Mila, did you say something?' Oskar brought his head to her face and she spoke again into his ear.

'Thule is going. We need to go.'

Oskar looked down too, and yelped. Completely

ignoring Papa's measured advice about spreading out, he scooped Mila into his arms and shouted to Sanna.

'Get Pípa, we need to run!' He stepped on to the ice, and when it did not creak, he picked up his pace, moving in steady, low strides, almost skating. Mila looked back over his shoulder, and saw Papa lift Pípa.

Cries from the others went up like gulls as the ice groaned under the weight of so many people. Thule was disappearing in great swallows. The white ice was as thin as cloth worn by washing, pegged out at intervals along the island's disappearing edge.

Mila heard a purring like a giant cat, and a clack of claws as ice splintered further. She saw the ocean exhaling a stream of bubbles under ice glass-thin. It was melting fast as Thule was fading.

And there was a man, gold cord still binding his ankles, gold eyes fixed on Mila's face.

The Bear was still alive, and he was coming for her.

'Nearly there,' panted Oskar, as much to himself as to Mila. 'I can see Bovnik.'

But they were not going to make it in time. Even if the Bear did not reach them, even if the ice held a little longer, Oskar was tiring. Mila could see Papa and Pípa wavering too, overtaken by some of the boys already. None of them were stopping to help, not with solid land so nearby. She was slowing Oskar down.

'Put me down,' she said.

'What?'

'He's coming for me.'

Oskar looked back and yelped, finding the energy to propel them forward quicker and quicker. But it was not enough.

'You'll go faster without me.'

'I'll go nowhere without you, Milenka,' he replied.

Mila looked away from the Bear's awful shape, towards Bovnik, eyes filling with tears. A shadow was moving across the ice, like a beetle scuttling from the shore. More joined it, becoming a swarm.

She blinked the blur away hurriedly and a shout went up from one of the boys running alongside them.

'Sleighs!'

Mila blinked again, and saw that there were dogs pulling sleigh after sleigh over the thick ice closest to shore. One was moving faster than all the others, and before it drew close enough for Mila to see the driver's face, she knew.

'Rune!'

The ice cracked thunder beneath them. Mila heard the familiar warning barks of Dusha and Danya as Oskar practically threw her into the bed of the sleigh before running to get their sisters and father.

Mila willed herself to stay conscious, feeling Rune's hand squeeze her shoulder gently as Pípa and Sanna leapt into the sleigh, Papa and Geir collapsing on top of them, their bodies a tangle of limbs.

'Oskar, take the reins!' shouted Rune.

But still, the Bear was coming. She knew he would not stop until he caught them.

'Rune, he's—'

'I know.'

She cracked open her eyelids to see the mage's strange, kind face close, moonstone eyes fixed to hers.

'I'm sorry I couldn't come with you. It had to be you who freed them.'

'What do you—?'

'It had to be you, so you could see you are strong enough. You understand? You're the guardian of the forest now, Mila.' His cool hand squeezed hers. 'Take care of it.'

'Me?' Mila's head swam.

'Look after Lunka for me,' he said.

'Rune? You're scaring me. Where are you going?'

'To the Bear.'

She gripped him desperately, but he pulled gently away from her grasp. 'This was always what had to happen, Mila. That's why I couldn't let myself be taken. I had to prepare. I was always the one who had to do it.'

'Do what?'

'This.'

Then he was gone. Mila forced herself upright, watching Rune's slight shape run as fast as wind towards the Bear.

'What is he doing?' shouted Sanna.

'He must have had all the flameberry!' cried Pípa.

'*Farash!*' yelled Oskar.

Mila felt a wrenching in her stomach as they set off. The dogs flew. Thule was wholly faded from their realm now, and the ice was breaking up and floating to fill the space it had left.

Rune and the Bear met with a crashing force that seemed to set the air shimmering around them. Surely Rune was no match for the Bear, caught though he was in his human form?

'Don't look, Milenka,' said Papa. He manoeuvred himself alongside her and wrapped his arm around her. But she kept her eyes on Rune and saw the mage throw a glitter of black powder at the Bear's feet. There was a flash of brimstone, a crack, and they both disappeared beneath the ice.

'No!' Mila tried to throw herself towards Rune, but

she was held fast by Papa and Sanna and Pípa. She raged and cried, looking desperately back, but the ice continued to break up around them. No one emerged from the sea.

'*Farash!*' cried Oskar again, and the dogs seemed to run even faster as there was another bone-shuddering *crunch*.

Two shadows rose over the ice. Mila gaped. Even at this distance she could see that one was a massive bear, and the other some sort of bird.

'A gyrfalcon!' Pípa cried. 'Mila, it's Rune's gyrfalcon!'

Mila expected them to fight, the spirits of the Bear and Rune, but instead they hovered, facing each other over the unlocking sea.

'What are they doing?' said Sanna, muffled beneath her sisters. 'Why doesn't he attack?'

The gyrfalcon was circling gently, the bear floating, mighty shoulders heaving. Finally Rune brushed the Bear's shoulder with his wing and the Bear turned towards the faded Thule. Despite herself, some of the ache in her chest was for him, watching as he followed his burning forest into nothing. His spirit faded, and was gone.

The horizon flickered as Thule and the Bear vanished into another realm, then settled. Rune's spirit lifted on the air, circling higher and higher into the blue, until Mila could not see it for brightness and tears.

Sanna shimmied down too, to lie on Mila's other side, and hugged her tightly. Then there was a pressing weight on top, and Mila knew that Pípa was stretching out over them all. There was a bump, and the sound of the sleigh changed from smooth ice running to a clogged, deep-snow hush.

'*Stuta*,' said Oskar, in a voice thick with tears.

The dogs stopped and Mila heard them panting, heard the soft *putt* of their bodies collapse in the snow. Another shift of weight rolled them all sideways as Oskar lay down, lacing his fingers through the web of arms so he touched each of them.

The sound of her family's breathing filled Mila's ears, and she let herself fade, like Thule, like Rune and the Bear, into nothingness.

Chapter Thirty

Name-Giving

Mila lay on a cloud, warm sun on her face. Her body felt far away and light as air. A hand, cool and dry as paper, settled into hers, someone spoke her name. *Rune?*

She opened her eyes. The sun turned into tickling fingers of fire, the cloud a straw mattress beneath her. And a face, familiar but aged, beamed down at her.

'Welcome back,' said Papa.

'She's awake?' There was a scrambling, and someone knelt painfully on her hair. Pípa hovered over her, eyebrows knotted and anxious. 'She's awake!'

'Not so loud, Pípa,' chided Oskar, easing her off Mila's hair. Pípa stayed bent over her, breath tickling Mila's face. She seemed to want to fix her face in her mind, to be sure she would not disappear again.

Mila blinked about her. She was in a small, light room. The walls were stone, their outer edges curved, and she realized she must be in one of the houses in Bovnik.

'My hand,' Mila said, voice coming raw through her throat.

'It'll be sore for a while, and you'll have a wicked scar.' Oskar held up his own hand, with the jagged line left by her crooked stitches. 'We'll match.'

'Where . . . ?'

'Bovnik,' said Sanna, coming to kneel at Mila's other side. 'Rune saved us. He gathered the remaining people of Bovnik, and when he saw the ice melting, he led the sleighs to us.'

'I remember,' said Mila, the ice crossing coming back to her. 'He . . . he killed the Bear.'

Sanna nodded, placing a gentle hand on her arm. Mila fell back into her body at Sanna's touch. The sadness spun through Mila, sucking at her like a whirlpool.

'He sacrificed himself. He's a hero.'

'You all are,' said Papa. His voice was warm and wonderful. She looked up at him, his blue eyes, his broad face, stretched wider in a smile that made her heart ache.

'What happened, Papa?' Mila reached out with her unhurt hand and he took it in his broad palm. Mila saw he was wearing his garnet ring.

His face creased, and a stifled sob caught in his throat. Oskar placed a steadying hand on his shoulders. 'I'm so sorry,' he whispered. 'I never meant to—'

'Tell her, Papa,' said Sanna.

Papa could not look Mila in the eye. He fixed his gaze at her chin. 'The day I left. I never meant to go for good. I missed your mama.' He stopped, chest heaving, taking deep breaths. 'I missed her so badly. I was angry with her for going, at the forest for not protecting her. I wanted . . .' He looked up at Mila. 'I wanted to hurt – something. So I walked. I walked for miles and miles, and suddenly I was at the heart tree . . .' He broke off. 'I couldn't see for anger. I just lifted my axe and starting swinging.'

Fresh tears came to Mila's eyes. 'But the heart tree, Papa. It was sacred.'

Papa hung his head. 'It was unforgivable. When he came, I hardly fought. I left my ring like it was nothing, gave up my axe. I deserved what I got.'

A part of Mila almost agreed. She remembered Rune telling her she and the Bear were alike in some ways, and supposed this was one.

'How did you know it was Papa in the tree?' Oskar was frowning at her. 'How did you know the Bear took him?'

'The Bear told us,' said Mila. She felt suddenly exhausted, though she had just woken from a deep sleep. 'He said that, five years ago, a man tried to cut down his heart tree, so in revenge he took a cutting to Thule, and planted the man as its heart.' She shuddered, remembering her father's wooden body. 'And his axe, I thought it looked familiar.' She glanced at Papa. 'It was yours.'

'Forgive me, Milenka. All of you.' Papa's face was wretched. 'I never meant to cause such harm.'

But you did, thought Mila. Her heart was sore, thinking of the destroyed heart tree, the forest caught for so long in a slow, wintry death. But Eldbjørn had survived, and now spring was returning.

'We'll need to plant a new heart tree,' said Mila decisively. 'And take better care of it from now on.'

'Of course,' said Papa.

'We all will,' said Oskar. 'The boys will do anything you say. And their families arrived from Stavgar two days ago. We can spread the word.'

'We've been feasting every day,' said Pípa excitedly. 'I've had candied plums three times already.'

'It's a wonderful place,' said Sanna. 'There are so many beautiful things here.'

Oskar reached across and put a hand on Sanna's, and Mila caught a look passing between them, as though

Oskar was stopping Sanna from saying more. Pípa gabbled on.

'They're calling us the spring sisters, because we burnt down the tree.' She snorted. 'Geir came up with it. You think he's clever, don't you, Sanna?'

Sanna blushed and looked down.

Mila eyed her. 'I have missed a lot, haven't I?'

'That's enough,' said Papa, semi-sternly. 'Do I have to rethink my promise, Pípa?'

'What promise?' said Mila.

'Papa said that, when you were awake, I could have my given name.' Pípa looked expectantly at their father, who cleared his throat.

'Your name,' he said solemnly. 'Is Agneta.'

There was a pause. Pípa wrinkled her nose. 'I don't like it.'

'It was Mama's name,' huffed Sanna.

'Well, then, she shouldn't have to share,' said Pípa, and Oskar stifled a laugh. 'Can I pick another?'

Papa looked as if he were about to protest, but his face softened quickly with amusement. 'I suppose a spring sister should be allowed at least that.'

'Rune,' said Pípa without hesitation. 'I'll have Agneta as my middle name,' she said hurriedly to Papa. 'But my name, if you don't mind, is Rune.'

Papa let out a long exhale. He reached out and brushed a stray hair from Pípa's face. Watching him, Mila felt a warmth grow inside her, a happy sadness so gentle it made her insides feel raw.

'All right,' Papa said finally. 'Rune Agneta Orekson. All right.'

Chapter Thirty-One

Home

Mila ate so many candied plums that she was sure sugar was running through her veins in place of blood the next day. The inhabitants of Bovnik had already begun to return in the time she had been unconscious, and it had been a magnificent feast.

The meethouse was carved out of the mountainside, and was five times larger than Stavgar's. On the walls were carved all the families of Bovnik, and they found Mama's name beneath her parents'. Oskar used his knife to write their father's name beside it, drawing a line between their parents' names and then another vertical line down. Beneath this he wrote his and his sisters' names so it read:

Agneta – Yelfer

|

Sanna Oskar Mila Rune

When he was done it looked like a tree with very

strong roots.

The room was filled with furs and wine and merriment, but Mila did not want to be around so many people. She missed the mage so much it was like a permanent headache that made everything too loud, too bright.

She, Oskar and newly named Rune snuck away early, their pockets full of sugared fruit, climbed up to the trading platform and ate them overlooking the waterfall, thawed now and rushing towards the unfrozen and endless sea. Sanna had stayed at the feast, laughing and dancing with Geir while Papa looked on sternly.

A small procession of sleighs stood loaded and ready to take them to Stavgar, and then on to home. Dusha and Danya were well-rested, the spring routes would be nearly thawed, and in such a large group the danger from wolves would be less. Mila felt a thrill at the thought that she would soon be home. And things would be even better than before, because Papa was returning with them.

She piled on to the bed of the sleigh with her little sister.

'Look,' Rune Agneta whispered, showing Mila her pockets. They were stuffed full of candied plums. Mila shook her head as Oskar came out of the kennel with some extra food for the dogs.

'Where is that girl?' said Papa impatiently. 'They'll set off without us if we're not careful.'

'Here she comes,' said Oskar, pointing, and Mila saw Sanna's elegant figure descending the stone ladder ahead. Oskar came to stand beside the sleigh and gently stroked both his sisters' hair, as though comforting them.

Mila looked sharply up at him. 'What is it?'

But he only shook his head, and Mila felt a rising sense of unease as Sanna approached. She was wearing Geir's brooch, newly fixed, and was chewing her lip.

'Where's your bag?' said Papa. 'We have to leave.'

'I . . .' Sanna's voice caught in her throat, and she looked at Oskar, almost pleadingly. Mila understood.

'You're not coming,' she said.

Sanna, eyes glassy, opened her mouth and closed it again. She shook her head.

'What do you mean, not coming?' said Rune Agneta.

'I – I'm staying here,' said Sanna. 'I'm going to stay here, with Geir.'

'But you have to come home. We came all this way.'

Tears spilt down Mila's cheeks. She felt as if she were back on Thule, all colour fading again as she looked into her sister's beautiful face.

'Exactly. We came all this way. And I want to keep going. The world is so big and I want to see it. Geir –' Sanna's cheeks flushed crimson but she didn't stop talking – 'he wants to see it too. We're going to pass a spring here, and then in summer we'll go south.'

She looked at Papa, whose face was still, as though he were a tree again. She kept talking, faster and faster. 'We'll come past home, see you all. Maybe . . . maybe we'll race winter so that it won't ever reach us again.' She drew a shaky breath.

None of them spoke, only stared at her. Oskar was still stroking Mila's hair, and she realized that he had known this was coming. She felt a flush of anger.

'How can you do this? How can you leave us, after all we've gone through to get home—?'

'No,' said Oskar gently. 'You came to get me.'

'Yes, but now we have to go home,' said Mila desperately. 'Now things have to go on as they were!'

Oskar shook his head, smiling sadly. 'Things can't always stay the same, Milenka.'

'You always wanted to leave us,' said Mila bitterly to Sanna.

'It's not about leaving you,' said Sanna, striding quickly to the sleigh and holding out her arms to Mila. 'I love you. I love all of you.' She turned to Rune Agneta, then to Oskar and, finally, to Papa. 'Seeing you again is beyond anything I hoped for.'

She reached out her hand to Papa, and he took it, pulling her close. She still fitted beneath his chin. They stood like that for a long moment, before Sanna drew gently away and raised her face to his.

'I want to cross oceans, Papa. I want to have adventures. None so dangerous as this one, though.' She laughed weakly, then caught sight of Mila's face. Mila knew she must look murderous. 'If you don't want me to go, Milenka, I won't.'

A bitter twist of spite went through Mila. She could tell her not to go, could keep her with her, keep everything as it once was. But Mila saw how Sanna's face shone at the thought of the journey. She thought of how she felt now, so far from the forest, as if her heart could not settle. If that was how Sanna felt, stuck in one place, Mila could not say anything to change her mind.

'Be happy,' she said, voice cracking. 'You have to promise to be happy.'

Sanna pulled her tightly to her. 'I will.'

'Will you come and see us?' said Rune Agneta, crying openly now.

'As much as I can,' said Sanna. 'And I will carry you with me, all of you. The way you feel about the forest, Milenka, I felt that too, for a while. And now I think I could feel that about Bovnik. And when I stop feeling it about here, I'll go somewhere else. I'll have hundreds of homes, maybe. But wherever you are, wherever Píp – I mean Rune – is, or Oskar, or Papa, that is my true home.'

'*Farash!*' The first sleigh started to peel away, through the gates and around the edge of the mountain.

'I love you,' said Mila, throwing her arms around her sister's neck, breathing her in.

'Always,' said Sanna, hugging her back, and Oskar, Rune and Papa joined the bundle. They heard sleigh after sleigh set off; finally, it was their turn. Mila did not want to let go. She looked into Sanna's face, and her sister leant down and pressed a kiss on to her forehead.

'Go safe, go sound.'

Papa held her close before jerking the reins. Mila twisted to watch Sanna raise her hand, and disappear from view.

Mila hugged her little sister to her as Oskar stood at the front of the sleigh with Papa, arms around each other's shoulders. She felt the wind in her face, breathed in the air, which had already lost its chill. Overhead, a shadow swirled. She narrowed her eyes and squinted. A gyrfalcon wheeled high above them, pale as moonstone.

A lifting in Mila's chest matched its wind-winging. Soon they would be home, and for the first time in years the green shoots would be raising their arms above the ground, the trees unfurling their leaves and tipping them up to the sun. They would plant a new heart tree, and grow the forest strong – stronger even than the Bear had done.

Soon they would be home, bringing spring.

Acknowledgements

First thanks always to my family. To my mother, who reads every draft and answers every panicked phone call. To my father, who shows me the wild edges of the world and tells me to keep writing into them. To my brother, for whom I wrote this book, because he is brave in all things, especially in forging his own path. Be safe on your adventures. To my grandfather and grandmother – I adore you with my whole heart. To O, and L, and most of all, N.

To all the Millwoods, Hargraves, Karers, Kakkars, Slomans, de Frestons, Cautherys, Furnivalls and Joneses around the world. Especially to my precious Sabine, and the gorgeous Tilly, Fred, Emily, Isla, Pippa, and nibling number 6 (name TBC). It is such a blessing to have you all in my life, showing me daily what marvels kids are.

To my friends, who strike the perfect balance between guiding me and leading me astray, and especially to Daisy Johnson, Sarvat Hasin, Katie Webber, Anna James, Kate Rundell, Kevin Tsang, M.G. Leonard, Maz Evans, Melinda Salisbury, Cat Doyle, James Nicol, Lucy Strange, Frances Hardinge, Lucy Ayrton, Laura Theis, Sam Guglani, Samantha Shannon, Abi Elphinstone, and the Unruly Writers. Thank you to Fiona Noble for your support and kindness.

Thank you to the Janklow & Nesbit team, and to Hellie Ogden, my agent and friend. You are fierce and wonderful, and I'm so glad you're on my side.

Thank you to all at Chicken House: Barry, Rachel L., Rachel H., Elinor, Jazz, Kesia, Sarah, Esther, Daphne, and Laura M., for your constant energy, care and support. This book was a labour of love for all of us, and thank you for believing in it even when I was mid-edit and starting to lose hope! Thank you to Helen Crawford-White, for another triumph of design.

Thank you to all the readers who want to come on these adventures with me.

Last thanks always to my husband, Tom. Thank you for the pep talks, the reading aloud, the constant inspiration, and the endless, endless love. What a tremendous thing it is, to get to share my life with you.

Kiran Millwood Hargrave

was born in London in 1990. She studied at both Cambridge and Oxford Universities, and is an award-winning poet and playwright. Her writing has taken her from the wilds of Canada to the mountains of Japan, but she lives by the river in Oxford.

Her bestselling debut, *The Girl of Ink & Stars*, won the Waterstone's Children's Book Prize 2017 and the British Book Awards Children's Book of the Year. Her second novel, *The Island at the End of Everything*, was shortlisted for both the Costa Book Award and the Blue Peter Book Award.

www.kiranmillwoodhargrave.co.uk
@Kiran_MH